# Bed & Breakfast
# & BONDAGE 2

## KATE ALLURE

ISBN: 978-1-7326957-2-6
Published 2018 by Kate Allure Books
Cover Design by Steven Glapa

# Rave Reviews for Kate Allure

### LAWYER UP

"The sensuality and sexuality are palpable…**4 Stars!**"

—*RT Book Reviews*

"*Lawyer Up* puts the sexiness back in suits and ties (especially ties) with a collection of sizzling stories exploring how bad a person can be in the bedroom while still keeping it legal. **Best Romances of August 2016**"

—*Amazon's Omnivoracious*

"Discovering unexpected second chances and finding love again. Every tale is unique and pure hot perfection…Read with caution — your hands may acquire scorch marks. **5 Stars!**"

—*Goodreads*

"Intense chemistry, great characterization, and a kinky page-singeing ending will have readers clamoring for more…all three stories pack an emotional punch."

—*Publishers Weekly*

### LAYING PIPE

"Seriously these two made me laugh, the playful nature, the sex rolled off the pages and Joe made Lexi feel great about herself. I loved the playful, witty dialogue. It's a quick and easy read and so light hearted. What a refreshing change to have a fun, playful book with two perfect peas in a pod. " **4 Stars!**

— *Goodreads*

## PLAYING DOCTOR

"Kate Allure deals in pure fantasy, a spirited diversion from the mundane and a chance to explore some of the most titillating "what ifs" readers can imagine."

—*RT Book Reviews*

"Readers will cheer on these strong women as they take the initiative, seeking (and finding) both sexual satisfaction and emotional fulfillment."

—*Publishers Weekly*

"Fun, flirty characters abound, and there's plenty of kinky action."

— *Library Journal*

"This book was smoking Hot! Being a nurse I can say I loved this theme because there are a lot of hot doctors and interns out there that you can't help but fantasize about..."

—*Goodreads Bookaholic GE*


## BED & BREAKFAST & BONDAGE

"Hotter than a steam room on a hot summer's day. Yeah that probably didn't make sense but when you read this book you will be craving the ice cubes for the cool down that surely won't come even as the last word is read."

—*Amazon Customer Review*

"Very sexy but with strong characters. Suspenseful where I was even worried about the bad guy...It's fun and entertaining."

—*The Booksage*

# Bed & Breakfast
# & BONDAGE 2

# Chapter 1

*~ wicked things happen late at night*

Lyndsey couldn't fall asleep. Afraid of waking her three friends, she lay there absolutely still, reining in the impulse to flop around in an attempt to find a more comfortable sleeping position. She was having a lovely time reconnecting with her friends on their long weekend to Napa Valley, but hearing about her friends' romantic escapades, while she hadn't had a boyfriend in recent memory, hadn't been exactly fun. It had roused the restlessness she felt lately, a feeling that might be called loneliness, if it weren't centered much lower than her heart.

Glancing at the clock, she saw it was just after midnight. With a quiet sigh, Lyndsey gave up and snuck out of bed. With all the wine she'd consumed that day, she should be sleeping like a zombie in the daytime — or was that a vampire? She could never remember.

Getting a little fresh air might help. Not wanting to disturb her girlfriends, she retrieved the dress she'd dropped on a chair and changed in the bathroom. Grabbing the room key, Lyndsey slipped quietly out of their suite, shoes and sweater in hand, heading for the cozy wooden swing on the veranda of the Tulip House B&B.

Stepping out the front door, she realized the sweater almost wasn't needed. While St. Helena could get chilly on an autumn night, it was beautiful out, only slightly cool. The moon was full and the stars amazing. Far brighter than ever possible in the sprawling metropolis of the Bay Area that she now called home.

It was a night for romance. Just not for her.

Lyndsey settled on the cushion seat of the wooden swing and gently rocked back and forth, gazing up at the Milky Way. The swing creaked slightly but not enough to wake anyone in the old farmhouse turned B&B.

The harmony of nature played a concert in the dark— thousands of chirping crickets and the occasional call of a bull-frog or wild bird. *Lovely.* Over that, Lyndsey heard another melody, muffled but distinctly not another gift from mother nature. Turning her ear toward the sound, she heard only the blur of many voices talking quietly. It was coming from down the lane, behind the tall hedge that separated the yard from the fields beyond. It didn't have the raucous sound of a big party. Why were there so many people meeting late at night out there in the middle of the grapevines?

Lyndsey sat back and continued rocking. Whatever was going on, it was a gathering to which she had not been invited.

She rocked and rocked, until she couldn't stand rocking— and ignoring the sound—one more second. She had to know. Curiosity may have killed the cat, but this B&B had only farm dogs and a human owner named Catriona. So, she wiggled her toes into her sandals and started down the dirt path toward the enticing enigma.

When she got to the hedge, Lyndsey was startled by the sudden appearance of one of Cat's canines guarding the entrance to whatever lay beyond.

"Hi, Peanut," she whispered. Lyndsey still thought it funny that this giant of a dog was given such a diminutive moniker. Once Peanut recognized her—they'd played ball earlier—he wagged his tail, and she patted him on the head.

Feeling dangerously sneaky, like a female Sherlock Holmes, Lyndsey leaned out past the tall, thick, greenery to see what the heck was going on—the full moon adding a sense of the mysterious.

And she abruptly reared back, the shock making her eyes wider than any deer ever facing blinding headlights.

Peanut continued to wag his tail as if everything was A-Okay.

Gathering her courage, Lyndsey peeked again, wanting confirmation that she hadn't imagined the wild scene—that it wasn't, in fact, a midsummer night's dream and she upstairs asleep.

And this time, Lyndsey didn't pull back, could not have, even if she'd wanted to, so shocking was its spellbinding allure.

Spread out before her was a tableau of oddities, shadowy figures lit only by moonlight and the theatrical-like illumination pouring from an open door to an ancient stone building. About thirty people stood clustered in small groups whispering to each other. Some loners gazed at the stars or walked around, stretching and flexing like high-strung athletes. One couple avidly kissing near a tree caught her eye.

"Okay, everyone, it's about time to resume."

Lyndsey searched out the direction of the speaker, and there illuminated in the doorway was the outline of a seriously-built guy who had an equally seriously-mesmerizing voice.

*Resume what? Resume who?*

It didn't matter. His sexy, authoritative timbre pulled her forward toward the fringes of the group, closer to where he whispered with another man.

She crept forward stealthily, like a curious cat, and this time her curiosity might indeed get her killed. Whatever these people were about, it was clearly a secret, furtive meeting. No one raised their voice nor laughed too loudly. But what caught her attention the most about the odd scene, was what they were wearing…or not wearing!

Some of them, mostly the men, were all in black, whether it was supple leather or shiny latex. The men looked studly. The few women who were dressed similarly looked over-the-top-sexy with thigh-high patent-leather boots. One lady even had a long whip, hanging in a coil off her hip. The braided leather looked like the real deal—something a cowboy might use—but it also seemed to be part of her image, her total bad-ass, take-no-prisoners guise. Lyndsey had seen this look before but couldn't, in the moment, put a name to it.

But that wasn't all of it. At least half of the gathered people were in various stages of undress. All of them were sexy, especially the women with high heels, midriff-bearing clingy tops, and micro miniskirts that barely covered their tight asses.

But what really shocked the bejesus out of Lyndsey—had she been a real cat, she would be hissing, hair standing out—was the fact that several girls and one guy were starkers, completely fucking naked! Standing amongst the rest, they were quiet but proud. No hunching over or attempting to shield their genitals. Occasionally, one of the leather people would fondle one of them, not a nice hug or gentle caress, but a rough grasp of private body parts, squeezing or twisting. The naked ones kept their faces down and didn't respond in any way to the invasions.

She skirted the group to see and hear better, now obscenely curious.

There were also some normal people in jeans and t-shirts and the like. However, what struck Lyndsey was that everyone there, no matter how they were dressed, shared a sense of camaraderie and something harder to describe, a sort of aliveness, a thriving energy that showed in how they held themselves and in their enthusiastic whispers.

She looked around for Cat, since this must still be her property, but there was no sign of her. Sidling ever closer, Lyndsey saw that the kissing couple didn't seem romantic. The leather-clad man had the woman pulled up tight against him. While he kissed her, he arched her awkwardly backward, and his free hand roamed across her body, fondling her nude form wherever and however he wanted, and she just let him. It was strange enough that this was happening right in front of thirty people, but it was even stranger that no one seemed to be shocked and, in fact, paid any attention to the couple.

Abruptly all the talking and action ceased when the same man resumed speaking from the open doorway. Framed by brilliant light, his outline revealed a body of Adonis-like proportions, but his features were indistinct.

"Alright everyone, break's over. Time to come inside for the next demonstration. I'm sure all of you, especially the ladies, will find this one most enlightening."

While his quietly spoken words were nothing unusual—if you ignored the fact that it was nearly one in the morning—his deep voice was hypnotic. Sexy and sinful, and something else undefinable that called to her, like the faraway rumble of thunder, the kind where you know that something of incredible power is coming. His voice tickled parts of her down low.

Everyone immediately started for the door, and Lyndsey paused, unsure how to leave unnoticed.

"Hurry up. Master Edge won't like it if you keep him waiting," a leather-clad guy scolded her.

"What!" She nearly jumped a foot.

Lyndsey hadn't realized she'd crept that close and was now on the edges of the surging throng. Her super-sized, bad-kitty curiosity got the better of her, and she let herself be swept forward into the stone building. Once inside, she leaned against the back wall, letting others crowd in front of her. The open door and escape were just steps away.

Lyndsey surveyed the large room. It looked to be quite old, with quarry-stone walls and big timbers supporting the wooden roof. A rustic and historic building, but whatever its original purpose, it was used for something outrageously different now.

She bit her lip against the gasps that threatened at every new freaky thing she discovered. There was a massive four-poster canopy bed made of steel and a luxurious old-world claw-foot tub, but that was where mostly normal stopped. Thick steel chains hung from the ceiling timbers. There were several odd black-leather-padded pieces of furniture and two human-sized cages, one hanging and one on the floor. And in the center of the crowd, a human-sized wooden X stood upright. It was all vaguely familiar—like she'd seen it before in another life or maybe read about it somewhere. Preoccupied, knowing she was trespassing and nervous about being discovered, clarity eluded her.

The person in charge, "Sexy Leader Guy" she silently named him, urged quiet, and the hum of voices instantly ceased. They obeyed him with the precision of a military unit.

"Alright, let's get started. I'm going to turn the floor over to our special guest, Master Johnson, but first I need to choose a volunteer. The topic is pleasure from pain." Immediately, all the naked ones stepped forward, variously posing like porn stars or liked humble servants with eyes cast down.

*Dungeon!*

Lyndsey thought she'd pass out right then and there. Sudden recognition of where she was, gushing into her brain—like a cold, wet mudslide, it nearly bowled her over.

This was a dungeon for…*what did they call it?*

Again, words eluded her.

Sexy Leader Guy laughed at the women posing before him. "We've got some eager beavers…except all your beavers are shaved clean." The rest laughed too.

Lyndsey searched for it, for the what and the where this familiarity came from. She suddenly remembered "that book," the one that had swept the planet. This was that, and they were about to beat some poor…*subservient?*

That didn't sound right.

Lyndsey started edging toward the open door, her eyes never leaving Sexy Leader Guy, who still scanned the plebes, seeming to search for the perfect specimen. He was a Greek Adonis in the light too, and she'd happily gaze at him all night long. His hair was the blackest black, and he was dark, his skin not tanned, but a deep tawny color that looked natural. He was tall, muscular but not too much, and super sexy with a daring air about him, like he could be a reincarnated pirate from the high seas.

Then his eyes met hers.

*Shit!*

Lyndsey froze.

His head tilted in concentration, his eyes narrowing. She took a big sidewise step, only a foot remaining before she could vanish into the night.

"Samson, please close the door," he requested.

*Shit, shit, shit!*

Her face whipped over in time to see the biggest badass in black leather from head to toe step in front of the door, blocking her escape. Reaching behind, he pulled it shut and crossed his arms over his chest, standing guard like a hulking doorstop.

*Holy shit!*

Her eyes swung back to Sexy Leader Guy, and sure enough he was still staring straight at her. The corner of his mouth quirked up, and he inclined his head just so. As plain as if he'd spoken aloud, he was challenging her: *What are you going to do about it?*

People started to turn and look back to see what held his attention, and she cringed at the pointed stares aimed at her. If she were a real kitty, she'd have bolted in a flash of fur, but human prey couldn't move that fast. A different leather man took a step toward her.

"Eyes on me," Sexy Leader Guy directed. Again, with sharp discipline, they rotated back around to face him.

Relief at no longer being the center of dangerous attention barreled through her like a windstorm, leaving her breathless and dizzy. Her pulse raced and her heart beat a rhythm so fast no drum major could ever match it.

But what now?

It was clear he'd done that to help her, and for that she was grateful. Although not sure precisely what he'd saved her from, she could have kissed him for intervening. And those lips of his were so full and alluring, she could happily kiss him all night long.

"Okay," he said. "Who gets to play with Master Johnson?" His eyes flicked back to her. "Perhaps someone new?"

Lyndsey lurched back, bumping against the hard stone wall, and he held her fast in his intense gaze.

After a moment, he released her and returned his attention to the crowd.

"You're all so willing," he said to the preening girls, "but I think I'll put it to the Doms. Which of your treasures has earned a special reward?"

Lyndsey's breath whooshed out before she realized she'd been holding it. More relief and, if she were honest with herself, the tiniest dollop of disappointment. She absolutely did not want to go up there, but having that gorgeous man pick her, instead of one of these beautiful night creatures, would have felt damn good.

The ones in power conferred amongst themselves, and soon a young woman, one of the starkers, was selected and secured face-out on the large wooden X.

Lyndsey tried not to notice or care, but Sexy Leader Guy had moved to a corner behind the structure where he could see both the demonstration and the audience.

Where, ostensibly, he could watch her.

Unable to control herself, she kept glancing back at him, and every time he was watching her. The corners of his mouth turned up in a wicked smile.

Then the demonstration began in earnest.

Johnson walked up to the wall of hanging implements—whips, crops, paddles, and other evil-looking gear Lyndsey didn't recognize. He ran his hand lovingly along them, almost worshipful. "Which one should I use?"

Restrained tight to the giant X, the woman whimpered. "Sir, I…I like the bunny flogger," her voice small and hopeful.

"Oops. Seems I forgot a step. First, *girl"*—Johnson pinned the restrained woman with a glare—"you know very well that I wasn't asking you. Second, we need to blindfold the subject. Slave 1 please take care of that."

Immediately, a tiny, gorgeous nymph bopped up from the floor, leaving another kneeling twin behind—presumably Slave 2. Wearing only a collar and marked on her forehead with a "1" that looked like it was written in Sharpie, she eagerly hurried forward to do his bidding, taking a blindfold from a basket and placing it on around the hapless woman's face.

Johnson watched approvingly. "1, why don't you pick the toy, too?"

Lyndsey snorted, surprised by how the sprite beamed at him, so grateful and adoring. Still, Slave 1 didn't really choose. Moving slowly past the various torture tools, her hand pausing lightly on one after another, her eyes were always on Johnson, seeking his input. When her hand landed on a short handle with several thin whips attached, he nodded almost imperceptibly.

"Good choice," he approved.

Slave 1 smiled at his praise, and it was breathtaking to see, her face lighting up like a glowing lantern of love. She grabbed the whip and practically ran to Johnson, offering it proudly with her eyes modestly downcast.

"Present," he said, his only thank you.

Lyndsey gasped at the way the girl fell to the ground before him, posing in a fashion that was both devout and lurid. Kneeling, her thighs were spread wide to showcase her shaved pussy. She arched her back to proudly display her naked tits. Slave 1's eyes were on his feet, but by the way she shyly peeked up at him, Lyndsey could tell the woman hoped that Johnson was looking at her and that he liked what he saw.

It was all so wicked. So naughty. So unlike anything Lyndsey had ever seen before or even conceived of. It shocked the hoo-ha out of her. Backed up against the wall, her sweaty hands gripped the stones with deathlike intensity. Her pulse raced with flight or fight adrenaline.

She looked at the door, but it was still barred.

A loud shriek drew her eyes back. The restrained woman writhed and tugged on her handcuffs, but it was the rash of red marks across her bared breasts that made Lyndsey cringe.

"You can use any toy, of course," Johnson noted. "But I've found that a cat-o-nine-tails works best for dispensing a broad swath of distinct stinging pain." His manner and tone were so mundane, he could have been demonstrating the best way to change a tire. "The more individual points of impact, the more all-encompassing the discomfort, making it more difficult for the sub to compartmentalize the pain and maintain control of his or her emotions."

"Wouldn't a cat with small hooks attached work even better?" asked a large woman dressed to kill.

"Not necessary, unless you want to leave a lasting reminder of the session. Myself, I don't like to mark the subject unless it's absolutely necessary, depending on their pain tolerance."

Noticing that the powerful woman didn't look convinced, Lyndsey glanced at the nearly naked man at her feet and saw several fiery marks on his back.

Lyndsey shut her eyes against the sight, a flutter of nausea making her gut clench—no way would she want that kind of pain. But something about Johnson's actions also called to her, like the dangerous lure of a siren's song, she was drawn back to the demonstration.

Master Johnson circled silently around the "lucky" volunteer, pattering her with the cat-o-nine-tails. Always striking a fresh, unexpected spot. Always eliciting surprised yelps. He was painting the woman in faint red welts as she writhed and pulled on her restraints. As his swats grew more forceful and frequent, her cries escalated as did her thrashing. Her body undulated as it twisted and tugged in a useless attempt to pull free. She cried out, "No more! I can't...*please.*"

But Johnson didn't stop.

Lyndsey began to fear this was some sort of cult. What if the restrained woman was a victim and didn't really want this to be done to her? What if they had some kind of hold on her? Unsure what she could do, Lyndsey pushed off the wall and took a determined step forward.

"Remember, girl, you can always use your safe word if the play is too much." It was Sexy Leader Guy, who's voice rang loudly, bouncing off the stone walls. "But remember with this weekend's special rules, that you agreed to, if you use it you'll be banished."

Both Lyndsey and the volunteer reacted to his directive. Quieting instantly and twisting in his direction.

"No, Sirs. I'm fine," the woman cried. "I'm sorry. I'll behave better."

Sexy Leader Guy didn't respond, his eyes were locked on Lyndsey. They stared across the space, and she felt his reassuring strength. Whatever the hell was going on in here, this man was in control and these people trusted him. They were safe.

She was safe.

Although their silent connection was probably only a few seconds, it seemed longer, timeless, and all the while the "play" raged onward. At first, the restrained woman tried valiantly to mute her physical and verbal response, but as lash after lash landed on her increasingly spotted body, she was unable to muffle the torment she was enduring. Her shrieks grew ever louder and shriller until somehow her cries morphed into something altogether different. Guttural moans emerged from deep within her that were earthy and erotic.

With the force of Johnson's whip, comprehension struck Lyndsey—these were moans not of distress but of pleasure. The subject's undulating body now screamed of arousal, not agony.

Johnson appeared very gratified by the woman's response. "You don't have to finish, of course, don't have to bring them to climax. This technique can also be used for punishment. You start with the pain, using it to build the sub's arousal, and when it turns to lust, build it higher, driving them toward climax. Then simply refrain from letting them orgasm."

There were murmurs of agreement among the power players, ones she now recognized as controlling the passive ones. Subs he'd called them.

"So, you're saying the punishment is the orgasm denial, not the initial pain?" asked one power player.

"Yes. It's no different from any other orgasm denial, but by starting with intense pain you can amplify the entire experience. Throw in some erotic caresses to start the sexual arousal, if needed. Trust me, I've had subs faint, not from the beating but from the fast escalation of arousal that follows."

There were nods of understanding from the powerful, and giggles from the subs, especially when things, presumably wicked, were whispered in their ears.

Lyndsey had a second devastating realization. She, herself, was near to moaning, her palms sweaty and her breathing fast. *It can't be true!*

But it was. She was undeniably aroused by this kinky exhibition. Her mouth dropped open and she moved restlessly, attempting to avoid the pull of this foreign but not entirely unpleasant yearning.

Almost against her will, her eyes slid over to the corner... to him.

Sexy Leader Guy looked amused.

*Shit! He knows.*

He winked. Then, eyebrow raised and mouth firm, he inclined his head toward the demonstration that had resumed.

Without a second's hesitation, she obeyed his silent command and returned to the unfolding scene.

"Obviously, after breaking the spell with our discussion, I'll need to backtrack now," said Johnson, "but given that our volunteer has earned a reward I'll take it to that more pleasant conclusion."

After retrieving a long stick that looked like something one used on a horse and another whip but this one made of soft fur, he resumed swatting the subject, alternating applications of sharp pain and soothing pleasure. Within minutes, she was back to moaning and thrashing, the increasing pitch and movement indicating ever-elevating arousal.

Mirroring sensations sweeping through her, Lyndsey was panting full-on now. Her libido kicked into overdrive, she could almost feel what the subject was experiencing. Unaware of what she was doing, Lyndsey stepped away from the safety of the wall and moved closer, wanting a better view, needing to know what it felt like, exactly. The shock of this madness had been completely replaced by an achy need she didn't understand.

Finally, the woman shrieked loudest of all, and Lyndsey watched, utterly spellbound, as a powerful orgasm took over the subject's body. She arched, bucking her pelvis, crying out, and thrashing for nearly a full minute. At last, the woman quieted and collapsed to hang nearly insensate from her restraints.

Loud applause erupted, the guests praising both the demonstrator and the volunteer. Lyndsey spontaneously applauded too, forgetting for a moment that she was an outsider, uninvited and unwelcome. She was totally caught in the moment, nearly longing for her turn on the giant X. Breathing heavily, Lyndsey wished for a release to the hunger that throbbed through her.

She slowly became aware of her surroundings, and mentally brushed off her unseemly arousal as nothing more than angst over the inhumane torture. People were milling about talking, and several were helping release the sub. The door behind her opened and a few people went out for air.

Her gaze sought him and, as she anticipated, he still watched her.

*Hello*, his eyes seemed to say.

He grinned and pushed off the wall, starting toward her.

*Oh, no. What is he going to do to me?*

Lyndsey panicked and bolted through the open door.

"Hey," called someone that she bumped on her way out.

She ran down the lane and was enveloped in darkness, but somehow Lyndsey knew that at least one person was observing her flight. She sensed his eyes on her but didn't pause to look back.

Once safely inside the farmhouse, Lyndsey took a deep breath to relax herself. She slipped back into the guest room, moving extremely quietly and slowly. She did not want to wake her friends, did not want to have to explain…*anything.*

She lay awake for hours reliving everything, exploring the erotic sensations that continued to pulse within her at the memories. Sexy Leader Guy consumed her thoughts. Who was he? Why did he affect her so?

A whole new world had been revealed to her this night, but it was a bizarre land, filled with frightening devices and strange hierarchies, where some were lords and some reduced to chattel. As arousing and intriguing as the scene had been, she couldn't picture herself ever naked and wearing a collar in front of a room full of strangers. Lyndsey didn't waste silent debate on the possibility that she might instead be a dominant, wielding rather than receiving pain. Her body's ardent reaction to the whipping made clear what type of sexual being she would be in this weird new universe.

*Stop this!*

Lyndsey slammed her hands down on the bed, then froze when her bedmate mumbled and turned over. Hardly breathing, Lyndsey reminded herself that none of it mattered. She wasn't a prude but she wasn't...*that*, either. Wasn't raised that way. Rather she was brought up to remain a virgin until she married, which she hadn't done, but still there was a wide gulf between having had sex with a boyfriend and being a sex slave.

Lyndsey rolled to her side and tried to put it out of her mind. Counting cats. Counting farm dogs. Definitely not counting spankings. Sleep was a long time coming and when it finally did, it wasn't restful.

# Chapter 2

*~ the next morning — was it even real?*

After returning from a quick walk, Lyndsey saw the fabulous breakfast spread in the B&B's dining room, and her stomach rumbled. Her friends, all old college buddies, didn't appear to be down yet, so she poured herself a big cup of coffee, needing the caffeine since she hadn't been able to sleep well after that bizarre midnight encounter.

Catriona came in carrying a fresh steaming platter of scrambled eggs. "Your friends are out on the patio behind the kitchen." She set the food on the buffet and said, "Try this and tell me what you think. I added some local cheese and fresh herbs from the garden."

She nodded and tasted a fork full. "It's delicious."

Cat beamed and returned to the kitchen.

Lyndsey heaped a ton of food on her plate and headed outside. Nighttime clandestine spying really got her appetite up, she thought, laughing at herself.

"There you are," said Carla. "We were wondering where you'd gone to."

"I just went for an early morning walk among the grapevines. So pretty around here."

No need to tell them, she went to peer inside a BDSM dungeon. But it had been locked up tight, and it was too dark to see inside and no one had been around—no Sexy Leader Guy. It was as if that crazy gathering had never happened. The strangest thing about it all was that she felt loss, like it had meant something to her somehow and now she'd never get to learn what it was.

"Earth to Lyndsey." Carla's hand waved in front of her face. "We were discussing what to do today, and Beth…you remember her, your college roommate…she asked what you preferred, but you were like, not home in there." Carla made another swirling gesture indicating Lyndsey's head.

"Oh." Lyndsey hoped her licentious daydreams weren't plain to see on her face. "Sorry. Yeah, um, I'm good with whatever you guys want to do."

"Great, then it's settled," pronounced Carla. "We're going to stay in St. Helena today and check out the local wineries and quaint stores."

"Sounds good," Lyndsey responded, digging into her eggs and trying to drag her thoughts out of the gutter.

\* \* \*

Three hours later they'd visited the local Napa Ranch and Meadowood wineries, and bought souvenirs from quaint shops on Main Street where they'd met some of the locals.

"That Doggy Heaven store was just precious!" exclaimed Trish. "I spent way too much money on Benji, but this puppy bowtie is just too cute! He's going to look so posh at the dog park."

"I'm hungry," said Carla, as they wandered around Bedroom Bonanza, a naughty lingerie shop. "I can't get over this sex store right here in nice-town USA."

"It's not like they're selling sex," Beth retorted in a shushing undertone.

"No, we don't," laughed a forty-something woman, who emerged from a door at the back of the store. "But if you want to see the truly sinful stuff, I've got it hiding in back." She aimed her thumb in the direction of an open door.

"That's okay," Carla laughed. "But I will buy this bra if you've got it in my size, 34C."

The sales clerk returned almost immediately with the merchandize in her hand. "Here you go. Anything else you want? Perhaps matching undies."

"Yeah, I think I would, if you have them in large. The owner of this store is lucky to have a good salesperson like you."

"Actually, I'm the owner, along with my partner," she said proudly. "Jen Bradley. At your service." She stuck her hand out to shake Carla's. She pulled the matching panties from a drawer. "Here you go."

"Thank you." Carla followed her to the counter and handed Jen her credit card. "Say, can you recommend a good restaurant around here. I'm starving."

"Of course. The best one for lunch is the Vine & Dine Bistro. The chef and owner is my friend Karen Williams. It's just up the street right next to the historic St. Helena Grand Hotel. The Farm Table is the best restaurant in town, but I'm not sure it's open for lunch."

The girls thanked Jen and walked toward the hotel, easily visible since it was the only five-story building in town. Arriving at the bistro, they peered through the bay window.

"Look at this super cute place," said Trish, while the others read the posted menu. "I like the vibe. Whaddya say we eat here?"

"All locally-sourced, organic ingredients run by two local chefs. Sounds good to me," said Beth, the most ecologically-minded of the group.

They entered the small bistro and seated themselves at one of the two large tables near the bay window. The other tables were mostly for couples. The feel was eclectic farm-to-table meets winery with some feminine touches—lace curtains and candles—that made it look perfect for a romantic dinner.

A young waitress took their order and brought them water.

"Is Karen here today, the owner?" asked Trish. "I want to ask where in the world she found those utterly cute wall sconces."

"No, ma'am," said the teenage server. "Karen's on vacation hiking the Sierra Nevada's with her boyfriend and won't be back until next week. Maybe you could leave your name and email. I'm sure she'll get back to you."

"Okay, great," Trish replied, taking the pen and pad from her and writing down the information. After the waitress walked away, she murmured, "This really is a small town where everyone knows everyone."

"Yeah, I'm not sure I'd like everyone knowing my business all the time," Lyndsey said, remembering the strange gathering from last night and wondering if the Bedroom Bonanza owner had looked familiar for a reason.

"Not sure why wine tasting makes me so hungry," Beth noted, digging into her salad after the food was delivered. "This champagne sauce on my chicken is delish," Carla said. "But if the owner is gone, who's manning the kitchen?"

"Doesn't matter, because whoever the woman is, she sure can cook. My soup's to die for." Lyndsey took another small spoonful and let the delicate flavor of the consommé trickle down her throat. "I would never have thought to use white wine as a base for broth. Mmm."

Lyndsey couldn't resist. She picked up the bowl and, holding it like a cup, took a long draught of the thin soup.

"You better watch out," Trish joked, pointing at her. "If you drink your lunch, literally, you'll end up under the table."

Laughter erupted around their happy meal, although Beth added, "Actually, the alcohol is steamed out in the cooking process."

"Come on!" Carla pointed at Beth. "We can always count on you to tell us what's what."

"No, I, didn't mean—"

"I'm teasing," Carla quelled.

"Look over there," Trish whispered, pointing at a man with a tall white hat on his head, his back to them while he schmoozed a table of diners. "I saw him walk in from the kitchen and he's effin' gorgeous."

"Must be today's chef," pronounced Carla.

Lyndsey watched as he made his way from table to table on the other side of the place. Then, he turned toward them, and she gasped. His eyes swerved to her, and he stopped moving, mid-step, surprise flickering across his face.

Lyndsey froze.

*Shit!*

It was him. Sexy Leader Guy, only he looked different today. Lyndsey had harbored a secret wish to see him again, but now that feeling evaporated like a breeze on a hot day. Intense eyes bored into her, heating her so quickly she wished there was in fact a breeze coming in through the open window.

And still he continued to stare. Was she about to pay the piper for her trespass last night? Would he embarrass her in front of her friends? Her chin rose fractionally upward and she stared back at him.

The barest hint of a grin appeared on his face, even as he subtly shook his head at her, his eyes narrowing.

Lyndsey gave ground without a thought. Her eyes dropped passively to her lap even as she wondered why she was responding in such a meek way. She heard his footsteps resume, and her gut twisted as he drew ever nearer.

Trish elbowed her, whispering in her ear, "Do you see how he's looking at you?"

Eyes still on her lap, Lyndsey shrugged, wanting her friend to drop it. She stirred her soup, distractedly.

"Good afternoon, ladies," his velvet voice as delicious as she remembered. "I'm Chef Damien Alaniz, and I hope you enjoyed your meal."

Her friends were quick to respond. Effusively and enthusiastically. Who wouldn't, to handsome man candy that could cook like a god?

He was professional and courteous, listening to their praise, and was even gracious with Carla who, as usual, needed to give her pointed opinion.

Lyndsey hazarded a peek, when she sensed he was engaged with Carla.

*Wow!* He was just as breathtaking in the daylight, but cuter. Way cuter! The white smock and poufy chef hat turning him from dominant and dangerous to sweet and savory. Approachable and charming, while he easily exchanged banter with her friends.

Without warning, his attention shifted to her. His easy manner held, but was touched with a soupçon of piquant authority, just enough to lock her spellbound. Lyndsey comprehended then that he'd been completely aware of her perusal the whole time. His slight quirky grin was back, making him even more sexy, if no less intimidating.

"And how about you? I genuinely hope that you found *everything* to your liking, Miss…" His voice had dropped to a huskier pitch but was seasoned with a teasing timbre.

Lyndsey hesitated, feeling unaccountably passive and unsure of herself.

Her friends, however, did not share her trepidation, all three supplying her name without qualm: "Lyndsey Taymer," they squealed in unison.

"*Lyndsey*," he repeated, purring her name as if it were sweet warm honey. "What did you think of what you've seen so far? Did it inspire you to want a taste of something new?"

She gasped and her friends giggled. They'd never seen her so tongue-tied before. While not the most outgoing, she wasn't a shy wallflower either, but they didn't know he wasn't talking about food.

"I…um…" She cleared her throat and began again, trying for a firmer, more confident air. "The *food* is delicious and the décor charming."

*There. What are you going to do about that?* She challenged him with her eyes.

Chef Damien grinned broadly. "Say…we've got some fancy new equipment in the kitchen"—his thumb jerked toward the back—"and sometimes I give, oh, you could call it a master class on how to beat carcasses until they're tender. A curious woman, such as yourself, might find a hands-on tutorial useful and satisfying." It was clear the offer was for her and not her friends, their chuckles filling the air.

"I, um." Lyndsey really had no idea what to say to that, locking her lips on what rose first to her mind…

*Yes. Please show me, teach me, spank me!*

But the feminist in her urged something along the lines of…*Get the fuck outa here.*

Which was soundly overruled by the exquisite clenching in her lady bits.

Before Lyndsey could take control of her unruly thoughts, her friends jumped into the void, telling him that they weren't local but that she didn't live too far away.

"But what about you?" Beth inquired. "Are you married or related to the owner?"

He laughed. "No. Karen's great though and we're old friends. She was nice enough to hire me to cook for them when I returned home a few years ago. Working toward having my own restaurant someday, and I'm perfecting my recipes now."

"Everything's amazing," the girls gushed, except for Lyndsey who couldn't wrap her mind around the fact that Sexy Leader Guy was actually here and seemed to be flirting with her.

"Isn't it delicious, Lyndsey?" Beth elbowed her.

She jumped. "Oh yes. Very good."

Chef Damien's knowing grin never wavered as he thanked them again for their patronage while staring at her. His glance back at her before disappearing into the kitchen made it clear that she was still in his sights. Lyndsey shivered even though it was a warm day.

She snorted with annoyance. Chef Damien or Master Edge, whoever he really was, had toyed with her, knowing all the while how much he was affecting her. A sigh of relief quickly followed as she realized that his teasing was very small payback for her trespass the night before. Lyndsey was beginning to feel like a ping pong ball, her emotions bouncing back and forth at lightning speed and flying off the table at times.

"What the fuck was that all about," Carla asked, voice low but demanding. "Lynd, do you know that guy?" She pinned her with a prying look.

Lyndsey shook her head, eyes down on the cold soup she aimlessly stirred.

"Yeah, he was a tad odd," said Trish, "but wow, he's super fine looking. I'd let him teach me to cook anytime."

"He seemed really into you," noted Beth, her regard thoughtful. "St. Helena's really not that far from San Jose. Maybe you should go after him?"

Lyndsey looked at the door to the kitchen. Yeah, she'd happily follow him, whether it made any sense or not.

"It's getting late," she said. "We should go to Sterling Winery before it's too late."

They agreed and were soon headed out for an afternoon of more wine tasting.

Unfortunately for Lyndsey, it was her turn as designated driver and, therefore, she stayed stone-cold sober. Without a drop of inebriation, she had way too much time to think about the mysterious, multifaceted Damien, a master Dom by night and cute, friendly chef by day.

# Chapter 3

*~ midnight calls and the nymphs appear*

Saturday night, Lyndsey lay in bed awake for hours. When she was absolutely sure her friends were asleep, she quietly rose and dressed. With nothing appropriate to wear, she'd left out the best she could piece together—a black t-shirt and skinny jeans. Applying fresh makeup in the bathroom, she snuck out of the suite and crept downstairs, alert for any sounds of wakefulness.

She knew it was wrong. Stupid and risky, even. But nothing could have stopped her from going back to the old wine house turned BDSM playroom. Curiosity was killing her, or it soon would, she giggled quietly. But she knew that Master Edge could not be as dangerous as he seemed, not when he had only teased her earlier rather than reprimanding her before her friends.

Visions of what reprimanding would be like in his midnight world filled her mind. Her pelvis clenched, and she sucked in a breath at the tingling sensations that coursed outwards from her core.

*God!* What was wrong with her that she'd have such a reaction to the idea of being spanked by a stranger.

She leaned forward to peek past the hedge, half hoping it was dark. Empty. That would take away the temptation.

Leaning farther, her head popped past the greenery and there it was. Lights blazing. Full of life. Full of strange kinky happenings. A session must be in process, because everyone was inside and there was muted applause.

Hesitating, Lyndsey stood there for a moment. Her good sense told her to turn right around and go back to bed. She pushed the thought away, quaking slightly with the import of what she was about to do. She tossed her hair, raised her chin, and started forward toward the open door. Not sure if she'd make it inside, Lyndsey strutted right up to the entrance anyway.

Standing just outside, she could see everyone's backs were turned away from the door. The wall of people made seeing what was happening impossible. She'd have to get inside. Sucking in a great big breath of air and ignoring her sweaty palms, Lyndsey stepped quietly inside and slid sidewise right back into what was beginning to feel like "her" spot. She let out a small sigh of relief that no one had seemed to notice her, or if they did they ignored her intrusion into their private world.

Her eyes swept the front of the room seeking him out, and when she found Damien, he was staring at her. He tilted his head a fraction in greeting, his expression neutral.

Lyndsey shrugged her shoulders and gave him a slight smile, her only way of acknowledging that she knew she shouldn't be here but...*please let me stay!*

The event was going full force with a completely-naked, blind-folded sub tied to a cross on display before an entire room of people. Lyndsey didn't completely understand what was going on, but the scene was providing vast entertainment for the laughing, jocular crowd.

Looking around, Lyndsey was able to discern subtle distinctions which, in her previous night's shock, she'd missed.

And thanks to surreptitious googling on her phone earlier, she had a better idea what was going on. The division into two categories was clear now—those with power and those who were subordinate to them. They had titles too: the men and women in black leather were Doms and Dominatrixes or Masters and Mistresses. The passives were submissives, subs for short, or maybe even slaves. Then there were Tops and Bottoms, whatever those were. Were you a bottom if your bottom was beaten? Or was it a reference to a *Midsummer Night's Dream* character? So many titles, and Lyndsey didn't understand the differences.

One thing she did know. Damien was the leader of all of them. That he was a Dom was hugely evident by the way he held himself, by the tenor of his voice, and that ever-present alpha-male masculinity that radiated off him in waves, making her knees weak. That he was a Master showed in the way the other power players deferred to him and sought his advice. Maybe one was a Top if they topped everyone else? It was confusing, although Lyndsey was quite sure there wasn't a Top in Shakespeare's famous play.

Again, she didn't see the B&B owner. She must somehow be a part of this, but Lyndsey was relieved, guessing Cat might make her leave the private event.

Lyndsey's heart started to pound when she saw that not just some, but all—every single one of the subs—were nude tonight. Male and female alike. Many wore collars and some were even attached to leashes. Tingles skittered down Lyndsey's back and she shuddered uncontrollably.

But one thing upset her most of all—the sudden realization that it wasn't disgust that made her quiver at the sight of naked human beings on their knees, gazing adoringly up at the one who lorded over them or crawling behind on a leash. What had shocked her most of all was the urge she felt to be on the ground too, looking up at Damien in that subservient way. Ready, willing, and unable to deny him any kinky depraved thing he might ask of her.

"Please, Sir!" the sub begged, almost crying. "I need it."

Drawn back to the unfolding scene, Lyndsey watched the Dom laugh and resume a slow circle of the restrained woman. "Maybe if you're very good, I mean very *very* good to me later, I'll give you some relief."

"Please Sir, I can't take anymore." She really did look desperate.

Lyndsey didn't understand what couldn't be taken anymore. There were no marks, no indication of any whippings, and the woman wasn't in some sort of uncomfortable contorted position. Except for the sheen of sweat, she didn't appear to be in pain or suffering physical discomfort.

The Dom held something in his hand. He moved to stand in front of the submissive. Although Lyndsey could hear a low buzzing noise, she couldn't see what the Dom was doing. All of sudden, the sub thrashed about against her restraints and moaned, the distressed sound reverberating off the rafters. The sound wasn't pain, exactly, more like someone about to have an orgasm.

"Yes, more…please, Sir!"

Instantly, the buzzing stopped, and the sub collapsed, hanging from the tight restraints.

"Master!" The long frantic wail rent the air.

"No," the Dom responded, his tone severe. "If I let you come it wouldn't be punishment, would it? You already confessed to breaking one of my most important rules, so you tell me...should you be allowed to come?"

The Dom stepped aside and faced the audience, and Lyndsey could see the panting sub fully now. The poor woman looked defeated. Her head down, she hung limp and worn out.

"No, Master." Her voice was so low it was barely audible. "I'm sorry, Sir. I won't disobey you again."

Lyndsey was aghast but again, not disgusted. Her pulse feverish, she felt hot all over. She swayed, as if she were fighting a river's strong current, lust washing over her in wave after rolling wave. While aghast about her reaction, she was too innately honest to pretend it was revulsion that conjured this river of roiling sensation.

*But why am I reacting like this? Why does the whole scene turn me on?*

She was an independent woman who put her career ahead of romance and sex. Ahead of men. It shocked, almost appalled her, that she wanted to be that person, wanted to be treated that way. But only if the man administering the punishment was...

Frantically, her eyes sought him out. Damien.

He still watched her with an intensity that burned her ever hotter.

He grinned and subtly tilted his head toward the cross.

Her mouth dropped open.

*He knows!*

Once again, Lyndsey realized he could tell exactly what she was thinking. Feeling. A heightened fight-or-flight alert kicked in. Trapped by his increasingly direct stare, she started to bolt, even as her gaze stayed locked with his.

His lips turned down in a frown and that stopped her dead. Disappointment or disapproval? Lyndsey didn't want either from him. Not about her.

She inhaled long and hard and turned her body to face him, raising her chin slightly.

*I'll not run. So there!*

Damien broke into a broad grin, and he again tipped his head to her. The erotic waves coursing through her were enhanced by the silent praise he offered…but Lyndsey didn't really like that his slightest approval affected her so profoundly.

Her chin notched up a bit higher.

*I see you and know what you're doing.*

Damien chuckled.

Applause broke out, breaking their silent repartee.

The presenter stepped forward. "So that's how you can effectively punish misbehaving bottoms, without actually pounding on their bottoms."

The crowd laughed—at least the power players did—and the applause grew louder. The Dom began to undo the restraints and the crowd started to talk among themselves.

"Excuse me, everyone," called Damien. "De Sade's sadistic presentation was…painfully edifying, at least for Janey." Everyone laughed again. "But we are running a little behind, so I'll put it to you whether you want to break and skip my presentation or just keep going?"

"Master Edge," someone yelled. "Let's keep going. I really want to see you in action."

"Silence," barked the Dom holding the man's leash. "Master Edge, wasn't asking you."

"That's correct, Dom Bleu, but," he looked at the chastised sub now fully prostrate on the floor like a slave before his owner, "I do thank you, Billy, for your enthusiasm." He turned to face the crowd. "Well, everyone?"

Lyndsey saw that this time no sub dared even look up, let alone voice an opinion. The powerful, however, voiced agreement that they should skip the break.

"Alright. Time for the long-awaited demonstration of my special technique for pain-induced orgasm denial. Since, as you know, I have no sub of my own, I'll need a volunteer."

Lyndsey watched as three unleashed women surged forward, while others deferentially inquired of their owners whether they might volunteer. Within seconds, there were five pretty, nude women and one male sub on the floor before him. They preened and posed, showing off their voluptuous or willowy bodies or, in the case of the male, his chiseled physique. All eagerly offered themselves to Damien.

Raw acrid resentment slithered, like a venomous snake, through Lyndsey.

She could almost laugh out loud at the absurdity of feeling jealousy about a man she hardly knew, about the mere chance of being punished by him in public.

*I must be losing my mind.*

Lyndsey watched as Damien—no he was Master Edge here—took his time to look over the ardent subs, giving each a moment of his attention, but then his gaze shifted.

Slowly, inexorably, toward an impossible direction.

The whole room tilted, landing in a dizzying angle, as his eyes slowly traveled backward through the space, over the tops of everyone's heads, until he gazed at her. His interest was searing and strong, like the thickest lasso—it circled around and caught her tight.

The pull was overwhelming and she lifted her foot to step forward.

At the last instant, she lurched back, and her head smacked painfully into the stone wall.

*No, no, no!* It was a silent scream. *I can't go up there.*

*Yes, you can,* he answered wordlessly, his cocky half-grin back. Damien lifted a hand and pointed at her. "You."

Even as everyone shifted aside and a path opened in front of her, Lyndsey continued to shake her head. *No. I can't.*

Her eyes darted toward the door only to see the huge man from the night before block it.

In the perfect imitation of the Wicked Witch of the West, Damien challenged her. "Going so soon? I wouldn't hear of it, my pretty."

The guard gave her a hard look and a curt nod in direction of the front.

Apparently, it wasn't that no one had noticed her slip silently inside the wine house. Rather, she'd been allowed to stay, because their leader had allowed it, had given her free entrance. Her gaze swept back to him.

Now Damien was collecting on the debt.

Practically shaking, her gut in freefall, Lyndsey inched forward. She felt everyone's eyes on her, their curiosity palpable, but she kept hers on the floor, embarrassed and self-conscious, as she forced herself to take step after step toward him. Her mind whirled with questions as she searched for what to say. What to do.

She glanced up, and Damien smiled, the look reassuring and friendly. It gave her the courage to close the last few feet until she was right in front of him.

"Hello, pretty girl," he said. "Turn around slowly and let me see you."

Without even a second's hesitation, Lyndsey rotated, tingles flaring all over her body wherever he looked at her. Radiant excitement like twinkling holiday lights fluoresced within her belly, making her quiver, while at the same time trepidation wrapped around her chest making it hard to breath. Conflicting emotions and sensations warred within her body. She couldn't possibly go through with this…whatever it was, but, oh, how she wanted his hands on her. Just not in front of an audience. *Please, no.*

Facing him again, pleasure flared within her at the dark interest in his eyes. That he liked what he saw, gratified her, but equal parts fear landed like a cold heavy weight in her belly. What would he ask of her? Would he let her go if she begged?

Master Edge faced the audience. "So, now the long-awaited demonstration." A brief round of applause erupted, as he turned back to her. "Up onto the spanking bench with you."

Lyndsey turned to her left and saw the metal contraption she'd ignored before, not knowing what it was. Her eyes swung back to him, seeking support.

"Let me help." Edge walked her to the bench, his warm hand firmly against her lower back making it mindlessly easy to obey him. His touch left skittering shivers wherever he grazed Lyndsey, her trembling increasing apace, but it wasn't a bad feeling. Instead, it was delectable. He eased her belly down on the slanted, padded surface and, without words, he indicated that she kneel on the lower pads.

Awkwardly, Lyndsey climbed onto it. His strong hands adjusted her body until she was prone on the slanted thing. With her back to the audience and her legs pulled apart on the kneelers, she was obscenely open to the eyes of strangers, even wearing jeans. Lyndsey never took her eyes from his, knowing that without the reassuring connection she'd probably bolt.

Or at least try to—she assumed that the guard still blocked the door.

Master Edge leaned down and whispered playfully for her ears only, "Well, my little pretty, who'd have thought a good girl like you would want a taste of my beautiful wickedness?"

"I certainly feel like I've landed in Oz," she whispered back, finally feeling a little saucy confidence in the knowledge that this handsome, powerful leader chose her. "But you might find that I don't melt as easily as the Wicked Witch of the West."

He laughed, a deep pleasure-filled sound, and equal pleasure surged within her. Still, Lyndsey was not sure she could go through with it. "Damien, I don't—"

"No," he responded sternly. "Never use real names here, not without permission."

"Oh! I'm sorry."

"It's okay, but we keep our lives here secret."

"Yes, of course, I'm…"

Her mouth dropped open and she ceased talking. A thick leather strap being tightened around her thigh stunned her into passive silence. Was she really going to let this near stranger tie her down and beat on her? Lyndsey's already fast pulse raced to the staccato rhythm of her pounding heart.

He started on the second thigh.

"Hey, wait," called a deep male voice, obviously a Dom. "I think you forgot a step."

"Yeah, she's still dressed," voiced another.

*Wait, what!* Lyndsey only partially strapped down, twisted around to see who was speaking.

"Off with her clothes," a Dominatrix yelled, her arm raising with the imperial emphasis of a Roman general.

Chuckles erupted throughout, followed by more demands. "She needs to strip!" and "Those are the rules."

In horror, Lyndsey watched the growing melee, and fear stopped her breathing altogether. She felt faint and looked to Damien for aid, but he looked annoyed. At her or them, she didn't know.

A tall, rather beefy Dom stepped forward. "You know that I don't normally allow anyone to see my slave's naked beauty." He didn't shout but his imposing voice rumbled through the wide-open space, and the others gave him ground. "But as you can see, I made my Casey strip even though she didn't want to. I did this for the chance to learn from you, a Master's Master. And you are the one who set these rules for tonight."

Nodding murmurs of agreement descended into unison chanting. "Off with her clothes!"

Damien had gone very still. He stared at Lyndsey deep in thought, his expression flat, unreadable, as the chorus grew louder.

With a curt nod to the audience, he stated, "Yes, my oversight."

He released Lyndsey's restraints and pinned her with a look that demanded obedience. "Take off your clothes. All of them."

"No!" Lyndsey's defiance burst loudly from her. "I can't do that."

A resounding gasp traveled through the crowd. Even the kneeling Subs joined the shocked mutterings.

*Shit!* Lyndsey hadn't meant to speak aloud, hadn't meant to openly defy their leader. She'd really blown it and she knew it. "I mean, I'm sorry Master Edge. I just can't." She bolted off the bench and headed toward the door.

"Where are you going," the guard—she dubbed him Hulking Doorstop—demanded, blocking her exit.

Lyndsey skidded to a stop in front of him. "I, ah...I don't belong here."

"You entered of your own free will, yes? No one forced you?"

"Um, well yeah, but—"

"The rules are posted outside the door for everyone to see. They state—"

"Rules?" The alarm and confusion overwhelming Lyndsey made it seem like she was hearing him through cold viscous fluid. Comprehension impossible.

Glaring at her interruption, Hulking Doorstop continued but addressed his words to the throng. "By entering this dungeon tonight, all submissives and slaves agree that they do so of their own free will and may not be forced within by their dominant. Further, for this night only, all subs/slaves give up all their rights, their clothes, and even their safe word, trusting that their care and wellbeing will be safeguarded within these walls. They do so in exchange for the special opportunity to learn from Master Edge and know that once they've passed through the door, they are well and truly slaves for the duration of gathering."

There were nods and grumbles of affirmation all around. The slaves stabbed her with angry glares, a bold one even muttering, "What makes you so special that the rules don't—"

The sub yowled, a crop having landed forcefully on her buttocks. "I'm sorry, Sir," she cried to her Dom, scooting over to kiss his boot.

Doorstop addressed Lyndsey. "You heard Master Edge. Strip. And start acting like a sub who knows how lucky she is to be selected for this demo." He took a step toward her. "Or face the worst punishment your pert ass has ever endured, and, believe me, correcting misbehaving subs is my specialty."

Lyndsey lurched back from him, her face hot. "I'm not a..."

The throng shifted restlessly around her.

What would happen when she admitted she wasn't a sub? That she'd trespassed? Lyndsey shuddered, fear clawing at her like Dorothy fighting the flying monkey monsters.

Instinctively, she turned back to Damien.

He raised his hand and silence descended, his authority as absolute as a king over his subjects.

"It's my fault," he said. "I invited this young woman but didn't fully explain the rules."

Lyndsey was dumbstruck. Master Edge had lied for her. She sucked in air, now able to finally catch a breath.

He looked at her. "You are free to go or stay, but know that if you do stay then all the rules apply to you as they do to all subs."

"I'm not a sub," she blurted.

He gave her a gentle smile. "You may not be aware of it yet. If you search deep inside yourself, I think you'll under-stand." He pointed to the door. "Now go."

Lyndsey stared at him. Even though she felt gratitude to Damien for saving her, she also wanted to rebut him, tell him what she was and what she most definitely was not.

At the same time a tiny part of her psyche laughed at her. If she wasn't a sub, why was she so intensely drawn to this whole scene? Why did she unthinkingly obey Master Edge, at least his easy commands?

Why, why, why...if she wasn't at least a little bit submissive inside.

Master Edge cleared his throat.

*Oh. Yeah.* They all awaited her decision.

She nodded once to him and turned away, relieved to see that Hulking Doorstop had moved aside. As she hurried toward the open door, she heard Damien tell the crowd, "It's okay. She's not ready, anyway, not for the red-zone of pain I plan to demonstrate tonight. If anyone here thinks they can handle it step forward."

Lyndsey glanced back and was somehow not surprised to see a surge of eager subs. Even a couple Doms stepped forward, offering themselves.

A shudder ran through her, the hairs on her arms standing out. Why would anyone volunteer for pain—red-zone or pink-zone or whatever crazy thing it was called? Lyndsey didn't care what he'd said or what he believed. *That's not me! I don't want that.*

Hurrying down the lane, she ignored a weird sense of loss weighing her down. It was as if she was giving something up, but she didn't understand what.

Lyndsey shoved the feeling aside, telling the chirping, croaking night creatures, and especially herself, "That's not me."

She fancied that they didn't believe her any more than she did, because somehow Lyndsey knew with all her being that Master Edge could give her something no one else ever could—absolute fulfillment in the form of an earthshaking orgasm.

# Chapter 4

*~ wanting what they have*

After finishing up his early morning shift at the Vine & Dine Bistro, Damien drove to the Tulip House B&B. He'd promised Catriona to clean up any remnants of the weekend's seminar, since the secret dungeon was booked solid with overnight guests for the next seven days. Even after nearly a year, he could hardly believe his good fortune in finding out on FetLife that a private dungeon for hire had opened right here in sweet little St. Helena. Man, would his old high school buddies flip if they knew what crazy shit went on down the lane on the outskirts of town.

Even better was finding out that he knew Catriona from his time in the L.A. kink scene. She had been a wild thing back then. Even though he'd never played with her, he had seen her in action on more than one occasion in various SoCal dungeons.

Entering through the side door into the kitchen, he saw her cleaning up from breakfast. "Hi Catriona, I'm here as promised, but I could really use another cuppa joe, if you have any left."

Cat smiled over her shoulder as she put plates into the dishwasher. "Help yourself. The coffee pot is on the dining room buffet, although you might need to warm it up in the microwave."

"Great. Thanks." He smiled at the pretty submissive and wondered once again why there were no sparks between them. It just wasn't there and they both knew it. He was glad for it, actually, pleased to have a buddy in kink who was local. If she were his sub, it couldn't be the same as having her as a friend.

"Hey, thank you again for letting me hold the seminar in The Burgundy Rose Dungeon. It's a great venue and everyone had a whopping good time." He winked at her. "I trust the attendees who stayed in the farmhouse were well behaved?"

Cat straightened and turned to him, sending him a genuine smile. "Perfectly discreet. I doubt any weekender could tell they were eating breakfast surrounded by a room full of deviants."

She giggled and he chuckled along with her, but Damien wondered about the one that got away. Cat wouldn't be happy learning that one of her innocent guests had gotten such a mind-altering eyeful.

*Lyndsey.*

His pelvis tightened and, once again, she filled his thoughts. The pale blond was about the only thing he'd thought about since she had first walked into his lair. And his mind was altered too. She was a beauty all right—pretty and curvy—but it was her other, more elusive qualities, that made the Dom in him stand up and take notice. And that wasn't normal for him, because he usually steered well clear of vanillas.

"Thanks for the coffee," he called, stepping through the swinging door to the dining room.

Lyndsey had surprised the heck out of him when she showed up again last night. It had confirmed what he'd sensed in her the day before. She was interested in kink and in him. He hadn't reach the pinnacle of the BDSM scene, a master of masters, without having a fine-tuned intuitive understanding of the needs of the women, and men, who served him. His reputation meant that subs threw themselves at him, and, frankly, the resulting largess had grown boring. Where was the challenge?

Pausing in the now empty dining room, Damien let his thoughts roam around his new favorite subject. He sensed a latent submissiveness in Lyndsey, a desire to serve and the hidden yearning that went with it. He wanted to be the one to bring those qualities out in her, help her to understand them and thrive. The idea heated his blood and filled him with something he hadn't enjoyed in a long time—a deep yearning of his own.

Damien filled a cup with the much-needed brew, but just stood there.

He didn't see her as a challenge, not really, believing she'd capitulate easily under his hand. What he craved was the chance to mold her unspoiled and beautiful submissiveness into the perfect sexual counterweight to his erotic dominance. Intertwine his dark demanding yin with her sunny serving yang and they'd both thrive. Just like the long-ago block of marble that became Michelangelo's David, she waited for a skilled artist to reveal the masterpiece that lay dormant within.

Damien snorted at his turn of fancy. What nonsense. He might be a famous Master, but, really, what did he know about her. Perhaps Lyndsey was merely curious. Perhaps she was a fan of "that book" and just sought more titillation. Quite likely, she was no more submissive than a large rock, something that could be stepped on, smashed even, but could never be shaped to meet his needs.

Sighing at the futility of it, Damien started forward, but the sound of a familiar voice slowed his steps. Lyndsey's soft tones carried from the foyer. "…so we're in agreement, we'll stay local again today?"

"Yes, I want to go back to Doggy Heaven and get that cute Santa hat for Benji," came the faceless voice of a different woman.

"And I'd like to try out that wine bar we saw on Main Street, the Sippity Doo Dah," said another.

Damien knew eavesdropping was wrong and started to turn away.

"How about we go back to the same Bistro," Lyndsey proposed. "There's a soufflé I'd like to try."

Damien stopped. Would she be there again today?

"Soufflé, my ass," came the mocking retort from, he guessed, the one who'd criticized his food. "You just want to see that sex god masquerading as a cook again. Plan to take him up on his offer to play a little patty cake?"

Damien chuckled quietly along with the unseen ladies.

They had absolutely no idea…but she did. Lyndsey knew exactly the kind of patty cake they'd play. And she wanted to see him again anyway.

"That's not it, Carla. The food was just very good."

Damien smiled.

"But if you all want to go somewhere else…"

Damien's smile slipped, turned into a frown, when it became apparent the rest wanted to try out another local place.

"It's time to go girls," ordered the snarky one. "We want to get back early since we're all invited to have dinner here at the B&B."

"Really? Who invited us," Lyndsey asked, sounding excited.

"Cat wants to try some new breakfast recipes out, and I really like her cooking. Plus, it's free food." The unseen others readily agreed.

Damien did an about face and headed back to the kitchen.

"Hey, Catriona," he called seeing her now taking a break at the kitchen table. "Rumor has it you're offering free food tonight. You know I love to cook, but even I like a night off now and then."

"Is that a hint?" She laughed.

Damien seated himself opposite her. "You know it is." He grinned broadly, now filled with good humor.

"Okay, but do you promise not to criticize my gastronomic skills. I'm no 'master' like you are."

The volume of their hilarity increased, and he leaned closer, "No, but you make a damn good sub."

"What?" From the doorway, succinct anger interrupted their tête-à-tête.

"Oh, Mason," exclaimed Cat, jumping to her feet. "I'm so happy to see you. I thought you were spending the weekend with your folks."

"Seems a good thing I didn't."

Beaming, Cat hurried, like the good sub she was, over to the imposing guy. Throwing her arms around him, she kissed him on the cheek.

That didn't quite mollify Mason. He still looked ready to fight someone, and Damien knew who his ire was aimed at. It was sometimes a problem when newbie Doms, like Mason, felt insecure around a Master, and it also didn't help that Cat and he were old acquaintances.

Rising too, Damien said, "Hey, ole buddy, nice to see you again."

Mason snorted, making it clear he didn't quite believe him. His arm slid possessively around Cat's waist. "What are you doing here? I thought your seminar was over last night."

"Ooo!" purred Cat, sounding like feline who'd been given a warm bowl of milk. Damien found it amusing that she could revert from confident businesswoman to sexy subservient with such ease. He watched her snuggle even closer, practically rubbing her body against Mason as if he were a scratching post. "Sir, you're so cute when you're jealous."

"I'm not jealous. I just don't trust other Doms sniffing around you. They only want one thing, and they're not getting that from you."

Mason had the self-awareness to look a little self-conscious about his not-jealous-outburst in front of Damien. "No offense, right, ole buddy."

More amused than ever, Damien replied, "None taken."

However, from the look on her face, Cat did take offense. "I would never betray you. " Her sexy purr had changed to a huffy growl.

She pushed away, but Mason dragged her back. "Remember what happened recently with that sadist from L.A., trying again to use his lackeys to book the dungeon. What would have happened if Lynch had succeeded in getting you locked in there with him alone?"

Cat firmly pulled her arms from Mason and stepped back, while Damien quietly chuckled.

"He didn't succeed. And for the record, there's nothing going on between Master Edge and myself. We're just old friends."

"You're too alone out here. You need me here making sure everything's okay. That's the reason I want to move in. Not to control you."

Unthinking, Damien snorted, and they both looked at him, annoyance in their expressions.

*Well, in for a pound…*

"First, Catriona, while it may be none of my business, if Master Lynch is trying to get you back under this control, then I'm in complete agreement that you need someone here protecting you. Lynch is a lunatic and you should take that seriously."

"There. That's what I'm talking about. Protection," said Mason, self-righteous conceit written all over his face. "I don't expect you to serve me 24/7, although"—he grinned lasciviously—"I would certainly love the *perks* that—"

"And second," Damien interrupted, "I'm absolutely floored. Still. I just can't wrap my head around the fact that my innocent childhood friend, former star high-school football player, and all around good guy is a kinkster. Who would believe it?"

Mason turned toward him, squaring off. Shoulders back and chin raised.

Would he start beating his chest next? Mason opened his mouth but Damien beat him to it.

"It's A-Okay by me. And I agree with you that Catriona needs a strong hand."

She glowered at him, arms crossed, from her spot in the corner of their triad. "And she needs protection."

From his corner, Mason nodded, crossing his arms too and looking smug.

Damien held his hand up to stop him from speaking. "And, I would be happy to train you to be the kind of Dom that can keep Catriona in her place."

"No!" they barked in unison, their emphatic rejection making it clear they didn't want him in the middle of their kink.

Damien stepped away, hands raised in surrender. Grinning, he added, "Mason, I'm just sayin' that I can instruct you on how to get *all* of her perks all of the time. On her knees, in her ass, in her mouth, however—"

"He doesn't need your help," Cat yelled. "He's all the Dom I'll ever need, thank you very much."

"Well now…let's not be too hasty," interjected a smirking Mason. "Perhaps some guidance on how to get full service out of my sub might be just the thing."

"Don't even think about it." Cat playfully punched him in the chest.

The three of them laughed together, the tension released.

However, Damien sensed the newbie Dom wasn't speaking entirely in jest. It might ease the distrust in their just-friends triangle, if he did train Mason to take a firmer hold of Cat's leash. To have that kind of power over another was an aphrodisiac all in itself—singular, satisfying, and sexy beyond comprehension. Even though consent to control was given by the bottom to the Top in a power exchange, if authentic dominance over the submissive could be achieved, she would be as fulfilled as the master. They would find a nirvana of passion and pleasure and unyielding partnership.

*Lyndsey.*

In his mind, he was there with her. His hand wrapped tightly around her neck. It might appear to others as if he controlled her, but in reality, she was eagerly yielding to him. She was…*his.*

The image of her the night before, in the dungeon—wide-eyed, scared, and yet trusting—hit Damien like the massive surge of a tsunami. It bowled him over into a vortex of hot desire, making him forget everything but her.

To his very soul, Damien knew what she was, a natural sexual submissive waiting to be controlled, waiting to be freed, waiting for someone to finally help her inhabit her true self. If he could achieve mastery over her, be the one to release her, they could, together, find that elusive nirvana.

Damien turned without a word and left. He needed to be alone. Needed to process his private maelstrom. In that moment, only one thing was clear. He would pursue this special woman. Get to know her, and find out what they could ultimately be, together. To do anything less was failure. To win, might yield the ultimate prize.

With Lyndsey, he might finally find a true, lasting partner.

# Chapter 5

---

*~ fighting for her*

As dinnertime approached, Damien grew antsy. He'd arrived early after showering at his place and changing into black jeans and a form-fitting t-shirt, his usual dungeon attire. He told himself that his disordered thoughts had nothing to do with seeing Lyndsey again. Masters, like him, controlled not just the subs around them, but also their own desires and needs. They didn't get their briefs in a twist over a woman.

No, it had to be something else, Damien concluded, listening for that newly familiar voice. He downed a beer at Cat's kitchen table and watched her putter about. Mason had a brew too, his glowering demeanor making clear he wasn't entirely happy that Damien was there.

Then Damien heard her. She and three other women came bustling into the kitchen carrying bottles of wine, one of them saying, "We've brought St. Helena's finest to go with your dinner."

They stopped short.

"Oh. It's you." Lyndsey stood there, surprise written all over her face.

He hoped it was a pleasant surprise.

The kitchen was instantly quiet. Lyndsey's friends nudging each other and grinning, but it was Cat's head swiveling over to pin him with a forbidding look that arrested both him and Mason. Straightening up from the oven, she asked, "You two know each other?"

Neither he nor Lyndsey responded.

The girls filled the void with various utterances along the lines of "Oh, yes, we met at lunch" and "the bistro on Main Street."

"I see," Cat said, but Damien could tell she suspected there was more too it. She'd agreed to the BDSM seminar on the grounds that it was kept secret from her regular guests, happening late at night and quietly.

Damien just shrugged. What could he say in front of the others?

Rising to face Lyndsey, he winked. Clearly, she hadn't told her girlfriends about their midnight encounters or their reactions would be less enthusiastic. He'd bet his best bunny flogger on that.

"Hi Lyndsey, nice to see you again." He used his sexiest voice and stood tall and strong, letting his innate raw power wash over her.

"I…uh…yes, it's wonderful to see you again," she breathed. Seeming unsure of herself, her hand fluttered in the air, and she added, "I've got wine."

"I can see that." He grinned broadly. "Let me help you."

He stepped closer and their fingers touched as he took the bottle. Her reaction was instantaneous. She stilled and stared at him, mouth dropping open. He knew then that she wanted him as much as he wanted her. That briefest of impressions, her warm heat, had sent electricity zinging through his entire body. If not for his tenacious self-control, he would have groaned aloud, aroused from just that split-second contact.

"I...uh," she stammered.

"Get a room," laughed the girl he called Snarky One.

For the next few minutes, there were re-introductions all around. Then Cat and her guests bustled around carrying dishes of food and glasses out to the dining room while the guys opened the wine the girls had bought at Napa Ranch.

Once they all stood around the table, Carla instructed, "You, here."

With seemingly no effort the girls maneuvered the seating so that he and Lyndsey were a little apart at the end of the large dining room table. Not private, of course, but separated a tiny bit from the rest. He didn't mind. Neither did Mason, by his satisfied expression. The only one who didn't approve was Cat, her eyes shooting suspicious arrows his way.

Damien shrugged again. There was nothing sinister here. He was just a guy, sitting next to a girl. Like that old movie, he might someday even ask her to love him. What harm in that?

Over the course of the dinner, he tried to draw Lyndsey out in quiet conversation, but she seemed tongue tied. He guessed it was because of how they'd met and what she knew and what more she wanted to know. She asked a few veiled questions, but Damien always changed the subject. He was already in too much trouble with Cat to begin explaining anything about his kinky lifestyle in front of her B&B guests, even if they were boisterously and tipsily entertained at the other end of the table.

Cat rose after they'd eaten their fill, and everyone complimented her again on the meal.

"It was delicious!" Damien repeated. "You don't ever need to worry about criticism from me on your cooking."

"Thank you, Damien, and thank you everyone for being my eating guinea pigs. I'm glad you liked it. Now I've got some local port and English cheese for dessert."

"Do you need help clearing the table?" asked Beth, starting to rise.

"No, I'll take care of that later. How about we go out to the veranda for our digestifs." When everyone rose, she directed, "Mason, why don't you escort the ladies outside and Damien can help me with the port."

Mason didn't look too happy about the plan, giving her a stiff nod.

Damien wasn't very fond of it either, when the second the door shut on them in the kitchen, Cat turned to glare at him. "You have your pick of every pretty submissive from here to L.A., and you have to go and target one of *my* B&B guests."

"It's not like that," Damien tried to reassure her. Quickly, he explained how they'd met and Lyndsey's obvious interest in BDSM, but Cat wasn't mollified.

"This is my livelihood you're playing with. One bad review and this place tanks. Any mention of sexual slavery, and I'll have the cops descending on me."

"Nothing like that's going to happen. You need to calm down…and maybe consider putting up a gate to the back lane." He grinned to lighten the mood. "That is, if you hope to keep nosy tourists from finding the dungeon. Obviously, the newly planted two-story hedge isn't enough."

"Come on, Damien. Don't do this. Choose one of our kind, a kinkster. Not her."

Annoyance flared in him at Cat's refusal to see his side. "You think it's easy, finding someone to feel a connection with? I've been waiting a long time, and—"

"I find it hard to believe. You're a famous dominant, a Master's Master, with a reputation for giving subs endless multiple orgasms." She snorted. "I've heard they can actually faint."

Damien let arrogance reign in his leering grin. He was damn good at what he did, but that didn't change anything. "So what. Subs throw themselves at me all the time, but I'm just a trophy to them. They want the fame and prestige of having snared Master Edge. They don't really care about the person underneath. Lyndsey doesn't know anything about that. If she likes me, it's because of me, not my reputation. And I want to get to know her, learn everything about her. With Lyndsey, I might finally have a truly rewarding and lasting D/s relationship."

Cat's expression softened a little, but she didn't concede. "Damien, she's an innocent. A vanilla who saw some kinky stuff that seems exciting. She doesn't really know anything about what it means to serve. I think you can find a special sub that's perfect for you, if you just give it more time. You're a great person and extremely good looking, which you already know. God, even I find you sexy and gorgeous and—"

"I knew it!" The angry outburst interrupted their argument.

Damien registered dismay on Cat's face before he turned to Mason, where the angry Dom stood in the open doorway. Mason strode toward Cat, letting the door swing shut behind him. "Is that the real reason you don't want me to move in? You want him instead."

He ignored her quick denials, rotating toward Damien. Fury transformed his gentle manner into a thunderous firestorm, his fists balled and his stance menacing.

Damien stepped back. Not wanting to fight his old friend and, especially not over nothing. "It's not like that."

Cat hurled herself between them. "Mason! It's only you I want." Throwing herself onto her lover, she hugged him tightly. "Please believe me. There is…no…one…else…in the entire world that I want but you. Just you." She kissed him hard on the lips. Arms around his neck, she practically crawled up his body to wrap around him.

Mason's arms went around her, holding her aloft, and he briefly kissed her back. Raising his head, he muttered, "I heard you call him sexy and gorgeous. Don't try to tell me you didn't." His rejected tone lacked a Dom's power, but Damien could hear another kind of strength there. The kind that some called a weakness or even an illness but one that Damien knew could bring lasting happiness. Mason was in love with Cat, even if he didn't yet know it.

"I'd be lying if I said that Damien wasn't good looking," said Cat. "But trust me. There is no spark between us, never has been and never will be. You're the only master I want in my bedroom…or in my life."

"Really?"

"Yes, really, truly. But, wow, you're turning into a regular control freak, a 24/7 Dom, if I ever saw one."

"Sorry," his muttered, his tone gruff, his expression embarrassed. "You bring out the beast in me."

"I like to think I bring out the best in you," she murmured, planting tiny kisses all over his face.

"That too." Mason lowered her onto her feet, and she stood looking adoringly up at him.

"Sir, I would serve you willingly, anytime, anywhere." She dropped to the ground and kissed Mason's booted foot. She molded herself into the presentation pose, kneeling with her thighs spread wide, palms up resting on her legs, and breasts thrust forward for his perusal.

Mason stared down at Cat, lost in her, and she gazed up at him, eager, ready, nearly panting with her desire to submit to her master's desire.

Damien backed away quietly. Watching Catriona turn compliant for her Dom, even one still in training, hit him like a punch to the gut, made it hard to breath. Turned him near weak with longing and envy. He burned for it. For the adoration of a submissive that wanted him for himself, not for his renown or his skills. He wanted the kind of easy connection Mason and Cat shared. He wanted the love he saw between them.

And he sensed that in Lyndsey he might find what he was looking for.

When he'd reached the door, Mason spoke to him, although he never took his eyes off the kneeling woman. "Damien, take the cheese and port to the ladies and make our excuses."

The supremely authoritative tone in his voice surprised Damien, as did the way he silenced Cat's objections with an unyielding frown and single finger to her lips. Maybe Mason wasn't such a newbie after all.

Damien chortled. "Sure. No problem, but Catriona, you'd better watch out. I think you've created a monster."

She laughed, eyes still on her Dom. "Yes, but he's my monster and I love him."

Damien picked up the tray and turned away.

Inside, his longing burned brighter. Lyndsey's beautiful face and natural sexuality would catch any guy's eye, but her other qualities were an even bigger bees-to-honey attraction for Damien. Her quiet manner masked an inner fire, of that he was positive. He'd seen the way her eyes ignited when challenged or teased. He sensed she was smart, and he knew she was curious as well as adventurous. Those were qualities they shared and could explore together.

She also had spunk and bravery. The way Lyndsey had turned up again the second night still surprised him, and he could hardly believe that she'd let him strap her to the spanking bench. How far would she have let him take it if there hadn't been the nudity issue. And just like that his thoughts turned to sex. He'd give anything to strip her bare and paint her tits with thick, sweet honey, and slowly, lovingly, lave it off. His gut clenched and blood flowed south. He wanted her.

He wanted everything that Cat and Mason had together, and he wanted it with the woman who waited outside.

*Lyndsey.*

He hoped she would want it too.

# Chapter 6

*~ I would take you over my knee*

"I wonder what's taking so long," Carla complained from her reclined position on a lounge chair.

"What's the hurry?" asked Trish. "It's a beautiful evening and we've nowhere to go but bed."

"Maybe I should go help," Beth said, starting to get up from the veranda steps where she perched.

"Really. Help?" Carla queried. "Cat's got two supersized guys to help carry a bottle and some glasses. I think they can handle it."

Lyndsey didn't mind the delay. Letting her friends carry the conversation, she sat on the porch swing, her foot gently rocking the seat, while she relived every second of dinner. She'd been mortified, at first, the way her friends had pushed them together, but it quickly became apparent that he didn't mind. His sexy whispers, often pitched for her ears only, were a fantasy all in itself, but when they accidentally touched as he passed a dish to her—well, that had been unreal.

"Oh!" she'd exclaimed, the heat of his fingers sending sparks into hers. His mouth had dropped open, and she could tell Damien was wildly affected too. And it happened again when he passed the butter.

He'd recovered quickly, murmuring *sotto voce*, "The first time that happened might have been a fluke, but twice makes me think we'd set the sheets on fire." He grinned, a lusciously lascivious expression that told her what he was thinking.

Sex!

Now sex was all she could think about. That and what wicked things he would've done to her had she been braver the night before. "The next time I won't back down."

His eyes widened. She'd accidentally spoken aloud and all eyes in the room were on her.

"Back down from what?" asked Carla.

"Nothing. Just talk." Lyndsey took a big gulp of wine. "This was a great choice," she complimented her friend. "I'm surprised, since it wasn't my favorite tasting. Don't you think Meadowood's was better?"

"I didn't. The best one by far was..." Carla could always be counted on to have an opinion.

Damien squeezed her hand under the table. "You're brilliant," he whispered right into her ear. The knowledge that they shared a salacious secret made her feel simpatico with him.

He didn't immediately let go, and she squeezed back.

After that, the dining experience changed from friendly coconspirators to something entirely different. Their mutual connection becoming steamier and more intimate. When his thigh accidentally bumped against her knee, she audibly sucked in air at the heat. Her eyes flicked to his and she saw heat there too.

The next time his thigh touched her leg it was entirely different. She knew he'd done it on purpose. There was a question in his eye or perhaps a challenge. Was he daring her to pull away? Whatever it was, she didn't retreat. Instead, Lyndsey did something entirely out of character. She slid her hand down and placed it on his thigh, while she joined with faux-enthusiasm in the discussion of the merits of different St. Helena wineries.

Damien acknowledged her move with the slightest of nods, a corner of his mouth curling up. The winery debate raged on, everyone apparently unaware of their private play.

When she went to pull her hand back, he moved with surprising speed to hold it in place.

"Not so fast," he dared in a barely-there voice. He winked at her.

His gaze switched to take in the group, while he slowly glided her hand down along his firm thigh. "You need to savor it," he intoned at full volume. "That's the only way to know what you truly desire or…to know which flavor you prefer."

"He's right, you know," agreed Trish. "And the way you keep gulping your wine, Lyndsey, you can't possibly know whether it's good or not."

Everyone looked to her for a response, and Lyndsey was clueless what to say. Or, more accurately, she was incapable of speech. Damien had let go of her hand and was now slowly tracing his fingers down her leg to her knee. His feather-light touch started back up the inside of her thigh, sending electric bolts of excitement straight to her pussy. She could feel his intense stare, sense the teasing glint in his eye, but Lyndsey refused to meet his gaze. She couldn't, however, stop the restless shifting in her seat.

Lyndsey did the only thing she could think of, her mind consumed be the sensations he was creating in her body. She grabbed her wineglass and took another huge draught, emptying it, before raising it to everyone in a toast.

Damien didn't stop the erotic torment, but he said, "I think what Lyndsey means is that we can each enjoy wine in our own way." The group laughed, and handed the bottle to him to refill her glass.

Damien didn't let up on his onslaught through the entire dinner, his fingers trailing back and forth on her thigh, and each time he drew a little closer to actually touching her sex. Almost involuntarily, she'd widened her thighs, but he never touched her there. Lyndsey managed to keep herself from panting but not from scooting a little closer.

Damien had laughed and noted for the entire table, "It's always the best when you tease it out, make it wait in suspense on the shelf until the time is just right. When it's so ripe, it'll explode in your mouth. Full of flavor and sweet beyond belief. Fine wine, like a fine woman, needs to breathe, and they both need to be handled with just the right amount of precision."

The others laughed, although Lyndsey couldn't help noticing the glower Cat sent his way.

Lyndsey laughed too, but her pussy clenched tight. He wasn't talking about wine at all. The idea that he would know how to handle her should rankle, but she had to admit that if anyone knew how to handle her…it would be Master Edge. She wondered if, by precision, he was referring to his use of a crop. The very idea set her off, sparking bright and hot, like the fireflies she could see tonight glittering in the dark among the grapevines.

Lyndsey slowly rocked on the porch swing and tried to imagine what it would have felt like had Damien caressed her…*there*. Holding her mouth firmly shut against the insistent moan at her lips, she could almost feel it, the gentle pressure, the perfect caress, the stimulating tease, the—

"Hi ladies," Damien announced, his tone full of jolly conviviality.

Lyndsey gasped, so abruptly was she pulled from her erotic musings. She looked up to see him backing through the door, carrying a small tray.

Putting the drinks on a low table before them, he said, "I have to apologize for Cat. She….has a thing she needs to take care of, but she sent me out to entertain you."

Nobody missed that Damien was staring straight at Lyndsey when he said, "entertain you."

"You know what, I'm feeling a little tired and might head up," announced Trish, elbowing Carla.

"Yeah, me too," said Beth.

"Come on, you don't have to leave," Lyndsey admonished, embarrassed by their obvious matchmaking.

Damien placed the tray with port and five cordial glasses on the table. "Actually, I'm hoping that Lyndsey might be willing to take a stroll with me. There's a nice path that way." He pointed down the lane where the wine house waited past the hedge.

Lyndsey's insides tightened. He didn't plan to take her inside, did he? With him. Alone?

He smiled down at her. "We'll just walk."

Keeping her eyes on him, refusing to see what her friends thought about that odd comment, she nodded and rose.

He smiled and stuck his elbow out. Returning his friendly grin, she slipped her arm through his.

"Help yourself, ladies," he said, turning away from them.

It seemed very old world, being escorted down the stairs on the arm of a gentleman. However, both she and he knew that the man leading her into darkness was anything but a gentleman.

Or could a Dom be a nice guy too? There was just so much she didn't know about the practice of BDSM.

She glanced back at her friends and they were watching her. "Have fun!" Trish called, and the rest chorused in agreement.

"But not too much," called Beth, ever the careful one.

He chuckled, and Lyndsey saw, again, how virile Damien was, his bicep hard and strong. The heat from his body, making her body warm too, making her tingle especially strong down low.

Glancing up at him, she saw that he was staring intently down at her as they strolled down the lane. She was glad for the nearly full moon which made it possible to see him even in the dark.

"You didn't tell them, did you?" Damien asked, his voice low, husky.

Lyndsey chortled. "No. Are you kidding. I doubt they'd let me walk off to a BDSM house alone with you, if I had."

"I meant it when I said, we'll just walk. You don't need to be worried."

A rush of disappointment, like cold water down a drain, washed away her burgeoning excitement. While she wasn't sure what Damien might have done or what she'd hoped for, "just walking" wasn't it. The thought occurred to her that she wanted a do over, a chance to experience that spanking from the night before, but with just him and most certainly not stripped naked.

*What the hell's wrong with me?*

Lyndsey was raised differently. Her conservative parents would flip if they found out she was interested in BDSM. Heck, they'd go ballistic just knowing she'd been in that weird place. That she'd allowed herself to be strapped down by a stranger.

However true that might be, it didn't change anything. Lyndsey still wanted to know more about what she'd witnessed. "Actually, I am curious about…" She gestured to the wine house as they passed the hedge and it came into view.

Watching him as closely as he watched her, she recognized the brief flash of excitement, before his expression became one of calm reassurance. "I'm pleased to hear that. Ask me anything."

"Can we go inside? Maybe you can show me what all the equipment does. Can we?"

This time, Damien's eyes flared with white-hot hunger before he hid behind a mask of calm. "We could, I've got the key, but I think it would be better if we just talked tonight."

"I guess introducing a newbie to BDSM must become somewhat tiresome."

Damien stopped walking and took both her hands in his. "That's not it. The truth is that I like you. I admit we hardly know each other, but what I see in you is a person who's curious, bold, and non-judgmental. The idea of introducing you to BDSM excites me, and I don't say that lightly. But I want to do it right. Does that make sense?"

A quick thrill, as bright and lightning fast as a shooting star, shot through Lyndsey, warming her in all those private nighttime places. That it sounded like he wanted more than a one-night whipping, maybe a lot more, also warmed her heart.

"I think I do," Lyndsey responded. Later, she'd address the crazy personal question of why she'd want him to beat her at all, that is if this thing, whatever it was, went anywhere.

Going for devil-may-care, she teased, "So, how do you introduce a person to being whipped?"

Damien chuckled. "Like porcupines doing the nasty, one does it...very carefully."

He put her hand back into the crook of his arm and resumed strolling, leading her down a moonlit path between the grapevine rows away from the wine house. "I think we should talk and get to know each other a bit, and you can ask me questions about the lifestyle. Why don't you tell me what you know already?"

"Not much." Lyndsey laughed, finding that she was self-conscious about admitting how utterly limited was her sexual knowledge. "I read that book, of course. Like everyone else on the planet."

"We call it 'fifty ways to get it wrong,'" he joked. "Although it did shake up things. Got people talking, which is good."

"So there aren't really slave contracts and red rooms of pain ..." She glanced back at the wine house, now almost out of sight. "Strike that. Obviously, there are BDSM houses."

"We call them dungeons."

"Oh, right." Now she felt even dumber in his eyes.

"And some do have private ones but most just rent them, like The Burgundy Rose. All very private and secret. But, more broadly, BDSM doesn't have to happen in a dungeon and it isn't one set thing. Everyone's free to participate as much or as little as they want. Play just in the bedroom or live the life. It's up to each couple to decide what's right for them."

Damien stopped walking and turned her to face him. "Tell me, what did you think while you watched the demonstrations?"

"I…um…well." Lyndsey stumbled on her words. She didn't want to offend him, but some of it was so out there. "It was shocking. Seeing all those naked people, kneeling so docilely, some on leashes, like pets. Some people had *all* the power while others looked like slaves."

"That's the most important thing you need to understand. The slaves really hold all the power, not the Doms."

"I don't see how that's true," her voice sharp with incredulity. "Shit! One woman even got whipped just for speaking out loud." Lyndsey regretted, only a little, her scathing tone, and Damien's implacability in the face of her ire only fueled it higher. "Double shit! They thought I was a sub. I would have been stripped against my will if you hadn't stopped them."

He smiled. "You're cute when you're angry."

"Would you still think it was cute if I was your sub or slave or whatever, if I spoke my mind like this?"

"If you were *my* sub," his voice soft but resolute, "I would take you over my knee and spank that sexy ass of yours till it was a pretty shade of pink."

The sound of her harsh gasp floated in the night air around them. She lurched backward a step, but Damien didn't let go of her hand. "I've shocked you."

Lyndsey was shocked all right, but she doubted he could guess the real reason. Damien's offer of punishment had made her moist and needy faster than the time it took to wet her whistle with a shot of whiskey. Who said aphrodisiacs were a myth?

Lyndsey shook her head. "I'm not really shocked." She wouldn't share even a hint of the fact that she might like such abusive treatment nor that she liked whiskey. It was so not a feminine libation.

"I can see we've a lot of ground to cover, before I can take you inside The Burgundy Rose. However, ignoring that, let me explain why a bottom has all the power. The sub, whether man or woman, gives permission to the dominant person to control them. It's an exchange of power, and can be revoked at any time. The sub also has a safe word that they can invoke if a scene becomes too intense, too painful, or for any reason."

"But that guy said no safe words."

"What you wandered into was an extreme situation. The rules for last night were highly unusual and, as you can imagine, that added greatly to the intensity of the experience for the subs. It also came with two caveats. One is that the bottoms only entered of their own free will, and second, there were three appointed watchers who would stop any scene the moment it became apparent that a sub was in duress, if for some strange reason the Dom didn't realize it."

"Oh. But why would a...lower—"

"A bottom or sub or, if collared, a slave."

"Okay, but why would anyone want to hand over such immense power like that."

"Tell me what did you feel when you were restrained last night? Did you like it or not? What did your body tell you?"

Abruptly, Lyndsey laughed, unable to stop her inappropriate response. "You know this is crazy, don't you?

Calmly discussing my reaction to being tied down before strangers and about to be whipped."

Now Damien laughed with her. "Good. I'm glad you can see the humor. It's a game and it's also not a game. It's about play and experience and sex. It's as serious as you want it to be. Or as playful."

His approval filled her with pride, warm fuzzies in her chest and a smile on her lips.

"But Lyndsey, you didn't answer my question."

That squelched some of her fuzzies. "Do I really have to say it?"

He nodded and waited, clearly not about to let her off.

"I kinda wish I had some of that port now." She sucked in fortifying air, before sighing out her capitulation. "Okay, I'll admit that before I got scared, before I was told to take off my clothes in front of strangers, I was enjoying it. I don't really understand why, but, yeah, I liked it."

"Did it arouse you?"

"Shit, really. I have to answer that too?"

"My cute novice, if you were mine, I would bare your ass right here and now and administer correction." His voice had dropped impossibly lower, coming out husky and, oh, so fucking hot that Lyndsey's insides melted into delicious, sweet, quivering jelly.

His grave demeanor suggested he was one hundred percent serious. "In the rare times that I've kept a personal sub, I didn't allow swearing. And, Lyndsey, I don't want that sweet mouth of yours used for filth. Only pleasure."

Great waves of dizzying hunger washed through her. "I don't understand." It came out a throaty whisper torn between desire and bewilderment. "Why does talk like that make me so…"

"Make you what?"

"I can't say…*that.*"

"Own it," he urged.

"It makes me hot," she managed.

He nodded, encouraging more.

She shuddered with the effort it took to reveal her obscene cravings. "It turns me on. Makes me want to yank off my clothes and bend the knee…to you."

"Yes." His whispered jubilance floated on the breeze. "Now you understand." Damien sounded thrilled and pleased. "That's why we do it. It turns us on. We like it. It's that simple and that complex at the same time. Human sexuality is confusing, but it's humanity's special gift and I believe in appreciating God's gifts."

"I see, at least I think I do."

"This leads to another important point about the D/s relationship. Actually, the most important thing. There must be absolute honesty between the participants. Misinformation when it comes to any kind of sex and especially extreme sex, leads to hurt feelings, wounded souls and, in BDSM, wounded bodies."

"Wow! I can see why you're their leader."

"Not really that, but I do have a reputation as a master of Masters." He sounded proud, and she accepted that it was something worthy of pride, no matter how secret it all was.

"Lyndsey, can you commit to that kind of honesty? If not, then I think you should wait until you're really ready, and maybe you never will be. And that's okay. This isn't for everyone."

He waited, quiet but leaning toward her. Even in the darkness, Lyndsey could tell that Damien wanted her to answer yes, and she found that she wanted to please him, that compliant desire yet one more thing to analyze. Later.

"Yes, I promise to be honest with you…if you promise the same to me."

"Of course, yes. I will never lie to you about anything, although you might not like what I have to say at times."

Sudden, surprising joy flooded Lyndsey. She leaned in and pecked him with a kiss on his lips. She hoped for more, but he drew back.

"Besides honesty, dominants give subs rules to follow. While it might not always seem like it, this is in the sub's best interest. If they follow the rules there are no punishments and pain can be used only for pleasure. If you were my sub, you'd have earned three punishments already."

"Three?" Even Lyndsey could hear the telling excitement in her voice.

"First for speaking with disrespect and, as I mentioned, for swearing, but the last was for lying."

"When did I lie?" she demanded.

"When I asked you if you were shocked."

"Oh."

"Do you still maintain that you weren't shocked or did you lie to me?"

Lyndsey's face dropped, her eyes on the ground. "Yes, I'm sorry. I guess you're right."

Damien's finger touched her under her chin and raised her face up to meet his eyes.

"It's okay. Was it shocking because my talk of punishment scared you? I don't want you to be afraid of me."

*Shit.* At least that time she'd said it silently, but Lyndsey couldn't let him think he'd scared her.

She looked at the handsome, earnest man before her and decided to go for it, not hold back. "Honesty? Okay, here goes. I was not shocked because you scared me. I was shocked because what you said was so fucking arousing. Oh, sorry." Lyndsey slapped a hand across her mouth.

The Dom gave her a severe look, but his eyes twinkled with merriment.

Lyndsey smiled back at him, before revealing her secret. "In my entire life, I've never been as turned on as I was when you threatened punishment. It makes me think that if I really did become your sub that I'd never follow your rules. I'd want to be punished all the time."

Damien's deep-throated belly laugh rang out in the night air. "Oh cute pet, you're going to be splendid and so fun to train. Last night, you claimed that you weren't a sub. Do you still think that?"

Now Lyndsey laughed. "I don't know what it all means, and my parents would freak, but if I were to tell you now that I'm not, you really would have grounds to put me over your knee."

Damien smiled and turned back toward the direction of the B&B. "Your friends are probably getting worried."

Lyndsey felt let down, but he was right. They'd covered a lot of ground tonight. Any more would be a mistake.

They walked hand in hand, and Lyndsey loved the feel of his strong hand on hers. "We hardly talked about anything but…you know. And I leave in the morning for San Jose."

"Would you give me your cell number and we can text and email. San Jose is not that far away, and I come down there on occasion for business."

"I'd like that."

They finished the walk in silence, and Lyndsey hoped he wasn't just talking as guys do.

When they got back to the verandah it was empty, everyone apparently off to bed.

"Damien, there's something else I should say," her voice a whisper against any ears within the open windows.

"Yes," he responded quietly.

"I'm sorry. I apologize for sneaking into your seminar, and I want to thank you for helping me when I got in too deep."

"I'm glad in a way that you did. Otherwise we wouldn't have met. And, honestly, I shouldn't have put you on the spot like I did. I knew perfectly well that you had snuck in, and as an experienced Dom I behaved badly. I'm sorry if I scared you."

Lyndsey giggled. "It seems that I like being scared by you."

The porch light allowed her to see his reaction. Damien stilled, concentrating on her, and his eyes darkened with lust as they settled on her lips. She shivered, not trepidation but edgy excitement.

Slowly, Damien lowered his mouth to hers, his warm, full lips fitting perfectly with hers. His arms slid around her waist and held her lightly, giving her the freedom to pull back or push forward. Maybe he was right. Maybe subs did have more power than she'd realized last night.

Lyndsey responded only with her lips, leaving her arms at her sides.

In truth, she didn't really know him. Was he Chef Damien or Master Edge or a mix of both? She wanted to learn all about him, but for now, the delicious press of his lips was enough. He caressed her mouth with his, sparking tingling fires throughout her body. When his tongue teased a corner of her mouth, Lyndsey moaned, her lips parting, allowing him entrance into her. Damien took it boldly, his warm wet tongue exploring her mouth, tangling with her tongue, and claiming her.

Lyndsey had never been kissed quite like this before—just mouths—and yet he was consuming her, making her weak with melting need. Her concerns about getting to know him better, only seconds old, were forgotten. She'd follow him right into the wine house if he would but ask. With just the gentle persuasion of his firm mouth, he'd rendered her submissive and willing.

Just as she was about to slip her arms around his neck, Damien pulled away. He touched his nose to hers in a too brief caress and stepped back. "Thank you, sweet Lyndsey," he murmured. "I look forward to getting to know you."

With that, he turned and walked down the verandah steps. And he was gone.

Feeling near desperation, she almost called Damien back to her. She took a step after him, ready to follow him to his vehicle.

Lyndsey grabbed onto the porch railing, her hands in a death grip, holding her in place. She might have learned a stunning, wholly-unexpected truth about herself—that there was the possibility that she was a sexual submissive—but that didn't mean she'd relinquish her dignity.

She watched until Damien's SUV disappeared around the lane.

If Damien sincerely desired her, he'd be the one to do the pursuing and the wooing. It might be a small victory, but Lyndsey knew it was the only power in her armory before she submitted to his dominance.

And submit she would. She had walked through a door into a new sexual universe and there was no backing out now, no shutting it away and pretending she didn't know. She wanted to explore this side of herself, learn how deep it went, and she dearly hoped that her teacher would be Master Edge, the one who'd pulled her into it with just his compelling voice.

Smiling at her astonishing self-discovery, Lyndsey quietly entered the farmhouse and silently went to bed.

# Chapter 7

---

*~ would she or wouldn't she?*

As they drove down the lane heading home, Lyndsey looked back one last time. She hoped Damien would email or text, but she had her doubts. Guys were like that. Hot one minute and inexplicably uninterested the next. At least that had been her experience.

Carla and Trish had a long drive back to SoCal after they dropped her and Beth off, but for now they settled in for a two-hour chat fest. Lyndsey listened with only half an ear, lost in the delicious memories from last night. Of course, the girls had wanted to know all about it when she came into the room, her hope they were fast asleep for naught. She'd already told them all she was going to, but for her it was an endless topic to be explored.

"You just won't believe what I found this morning." Trish's charged interjection invaded her private fog. "I went for one of Lyndsey's early-morning wake-up walks, and I went down the lane past that giant hedge."

Yanked fully out of her dreamy musings, Lyndsey hung on Trish's every word while pretending mild interest.

Trish turned around to look at Beth and her in the back seat, wanting to make sure they were listening. "Once I got past the hedge, there is this quaint stone building, an old wine house or something. The door was open so I peered inside. You wouldn't believe it. BDSM equipment filled the entire place!"

"Wait," exclaimed Beth, "You're joking, right?"

"The door was open and Cat was cleaning. As soon as she saw me, she hurried over and stepped through the door, shutting it behind her. Said it was her private art studio, but that was a lot of nonsense."

Not understanding exactly why, Lyndsey wanted to protect the B&B's secret. "Maybe it was her studio. What a wonderful place to—"

"I know kink when I see it. There was a St. Andrew's Cross right in the middle of the room, and spanking benches and other stuff. It was a fully-stocked BDSM dungeon."

Lyndsey opened her mouth, but Carla beat her to it, her tone so cutting it could slice ice, "You've got to be kidding. That's so, been there, done that. I'm really disappointed in Cat. I thought her entire operation was the jam. So trendy and earth aware, with her gardens and new age-y ideas. But that red room of pain stuff is so over. As if we women really want to serve men."

"Yuck," chimed in Beth.

"I dunno," responded Trish, "kneeling for a guy in that luxurious and naughty place, it might be kinda hot."

"No, it's over. Passé," snapped Carla. "Polyamory is the next big thing. Metro-sexuality and all that stuff."

The girls launched into an animated debate of what that all meant, but Lyndsey stayed out of it. She was too busy worrying.

*What is wrong with me?*

The idea of being tied up and spanked, still aroused her even now in the light of day. *Yikes!* Her parents would be apoplectic just knowing she'd watched a scene, let alone contemplated participating.

"You're awfully quiet, Lynd," Carla queried, interrupting her internal debate.

"Just a little tired. Anyway, I haven't had a boyfriend in over a year, let alone more than one at a time or a girlfriend either. What could I possibly add to this conversation."

Trish grinned. "I think our friend here has cooking on the brain. I would, if it were me. That guy is sex on a stick."

"What the hell does that even mean?" Carla threw Trish an exasperated look, before switching to the rearview mirror, pinning Lyndsey with a look. "And you. Not fair at all. You didn't give us a single spicy detail."

Alarm seized Lyndsey. She needed to stop this line of questioning before inadvertently saying the wrong thing. "There was nothing to tell. Really. We went for a walk and I learned a lot about his hometown of St. Helena." She'd surreptitiously crossed her fingers at the small lie, but there was no way she was going to explain that... *and, oh by the way, he's a Dom and the thought of serving him makes me wet.* Especially not after the way Carla had dissed BDSM.

"Well, he's some fine man-candy. Too bad he lives so far away," Trish mourned.

"But maybe you'll meet someone just like him in San Jose." Beth always the group's optimist.

Lyndsey's friends were her friends because they were unfailingly supportive. They launched into an enthusiastic discussion of how she could meet more guys in her new city, and she responded when appropriate. A corner of her mind, however, kept chewing on the topic of kink, like a dog chews on an old shoe, worrying it, dropping it, and returning to it periodically until the object is soggy, tattered, and unrecognizable. Until Lyndsey, wasn't sure anymore what she felt about BDSM.

Carla had, unawares, managed to plant major doubts in her mind about pursuing Damien. With him came kink and with that her subservience, not something she could ever explain to her friends and most definitely not to her parents. All that made perfect logical sense, but her heart and her gut and her more private parts disagreed. They vigorously urged—go for it, and while you're at it, let him spank you with that old shoe too.

As she waved goodbye to her friends from the curb in front of her apartment, Lyndsey wondered what she'd do if Damien texted her. Ignore it or respond.

*Who am I kidding.* She'd respond as fast her thumbs could type. That was the only thing about any of this that Lyndsey knew with any certainty.

She didn't have to wait long either. That night around bedtime, her phone buzzed with message from Damien. "Welcome home. I enjoyed our walk last night and the goodbye too."

Lyndsey smiled and sent him a…☺.

# Chapter 8

*~ three weeks later*

"Would you like a refill," Damien asked, holding up the bottle of St. Helena's finest sparkling wine. Lyndsey smiled and held her glass aloft.

She could hardly believe how well their first date was going. She'd driven up Friday after work and met him at the Vine & Dine late in the evening. It was closed now and they were dining alone. He'd changed into his usual black t-shirt and jeans. The wait staff gone and the lights turned low, he had appeared to be thrilled by her arrival, welcoming her with a bouquet of roses and a lingering kiss. They'd dined by candlelight at a corner table for two on a delicious dish he'd whipped up just for her. Lyndsey felt spoiled and special and desired, and that warmed her long dormant heart.

It seemed like she'd known him much longer than three short weeks. Because they'd talked almost nightly for hours and hours on the phone about everything and nothing, there wasn't a lot of getting to know each other discourse left. Instead they'd conversed this evening about their hopes and dreams for the future, for their careers, and about more personal issues like family and a desire for children someday. It made Lyndsey happy knowing there weren't any deal breakers to topple their budding relationship.

However, there was one subject they had somehow not discussed.

BDSM.

For Lyndsey, it was becoming a great-big white elephant, the blaring questions like the trumpeting of said beast loud in her mind.

When would he talk about it?

What would he expect of her?

Just how much would she have to debase herself?

Now that time had passed, Lyndsey was pretty convinced that she wasn't a real submissive. She'd helped her small company negotiate a great deal on benefits this week. She'd earned the CEO's thanks and even a raise and was thinking of upgrading her car. She was a successful career woman, not some docile sexual plaything.

It was possible that the strange magic of the gathering where she'd first met Damien, combined with all the wine she'd consumed and the novelty, had warped her thinking. The erotic sensations she'd experienced so profoundly had faded to nothing, now only hollow memories. Lyndsey worried that it was all a mirage, and not who she was at all.

But Damien was no mirage. He might be killing her with kindness tonight, but the underlying strength she sensed in him, his dominant personality, was ever present. Sooner or later he'd be expecting her to turn submissive. She wasn't at all sure she could do it.

"Earth to Lyndsey!" Damien called gently, leaning so close to her that they practically touched.

"Oh!" The exclamation came out breathy and ultra-feminine. Her spontaneous reaction to him hadn't changed. "What did you say?"

"You're a million miles away. Everything okay?"

"Yes, sorry. Just, you know, stuff on my mind."

"Please tell me. I'd like to help if I can." He looked and sounded sincere, but how could Lyndsey say that it was him and his need to dominate that was the problem. But if she didn't raise the question, she might as well go home.

"What makes you so sure I'm a submissive?" she blurted, her tenor tinged with resentment. "What if I'm not. Then what?"

Damien reared back, looking surprised.

"I'm sorry," she said, reaching across to touch his hand where it lay on the table, resting on the stem of his champagne flute. "That came out harsher than I meant. It's just, well, we've talked about everything else but that."

The look on his face changed to one of understanding and even a little condescension, she noted with mild irritation.

"Lyndsey, I was waiting for you to bring it up. I didn't want to make this evening all about that. I thought that when you were ready, you would raise the subject."

"I didn't realize."

"The last time we were together you wanted to go inside the dungeon, even suggested we check out the equipment. I had no idea you were having second thoughts."

"It's not that, exactly. But why are you so sure I'm a... what did you call it?"

"A natural sexual submissive, which just means you instinctively want to be dominated in the bedroom. It's nothing to be ashamed of. In fact, I guess that the majority of women like it when a man takes charge there, at least some of the time."

"Hmmm." She wasn't convinced.

"I really like you, Lyndsey, but I have to be honest too. I am a dominant when it comes to sex. I even tend toward that outside the bedroom, but can adjust when necessary. It's who I am." He sighed. "As for why I think you're a sub. I have years of experience. I've had women come on to me claiming to be that, wanting a chance with The Master. I could always tell when it wasn't their true nature, just as I can sense when it is."

Lyndsey fell back on her usual stall, downing the remains of her champagne. She held the flute out for more.

Damien shook his head. "I think you've had enough." His tone had changed, it carried the full weighty power of his Dom voice.

"*Really.* You're going to tell me how much I can drink now?" She reached for the bottle.

"If you were mine…*when* you're mine, I'll make sure you don't over drink and end up sick the next day. Just as I'd hope you would watch out for me."

That made sense, even if she didn't like it. Like a sludge-filled sink, Lyndsey's umbrage drained away slowly, leaving behind grudging deference. She wanted to wash that clean too, but it stubbornly remained.

"But," Damien added in all seriousness, "I'd take you over my knee for speaking so disrespectfully." His pronouncement landed like a sharp swat to her ass in the quiet room.

Lyndsey sucked in air, sitting straighter and clenching her hands.

Damien raised an eyebrow, and she knew that the provoking man was fully cognizant of the commotion he'd caused within her body, her nipples tightening and her pussy pulsing. Her fingers grasped the chair to hold her in place. She adamantly refused to squirm before him.

"Lyndsey, we can move as slowly as you want. I'm in no rush. I like you and want to get to know you."

"I like you too!" she responded and meant it. It was clear that the proverbial ball was in her court, but it was a game she didn't know how to play. Didn't know the rules any more than she understood the equipment needed to play it.

"Could we, maybe…" Her voice was way too timid. She cleared her throat and forced a more confident tone. "I would like to go to The Burgundy Rose now so that I can ask you questions about the things I saw there. But, you know, that's all. Just talk."

"It would be my pleasure," Damien responded. His face was a near perfect mask of calm sincerity, except for the flash of hunger she glimpsed before he could cover it. Lyndsey remembered the sense of power she'd felt before. That she could create such need in a man who was always so in control was its own form of dominance. Could she bring him to his knees, not to submit, but to worship her in his own fashion?

She helped him clean up the dishes and close up the restaurant, and followed him in her car out to Tulip House B&B. They parked and greeted Peanut and Gringo, who seemed to know Damien well, wagging their tails and dancing about. It was late and everyone was asleep, but she found a note and the key to her room in the entryway, and Damien carried her overnight bag up to the room.

Finally, hand in hand, they walked down the lane to the dungeon.

"I booked it tonight," he said, "in case you wanted the chance to see it again without a room full of kinksters."

"Thanks," she said, as they approached the wine house, that stood dark and looming in the black moonless night.

Now that the moment was here, Lyndsey's stomach dropped and her shoulders tensed, as if she'd worked a six-hour shift in front of her computer. She hoped Damien couldn't feel how sweaty her palms had grown. To cover, Lyndsey started babbling about how much she liked wine and how pretty the wine house was in the daylight and anything else she could think of other than what waited inside.

"Slow down," he laughed, unlocking the door. "You're as excited as sub on Christmas morning, one who's getting her first ever candy cane-ing."

"That's not a real thing!" Lyndsey laughed, some of the tightness in her back easing. "Is it?"

Damien smiled mysteriously. "The holiday's just around the corner, so you won't wait long to find out."

Lyndsey signed. "I'm sorry. I guess I'm a little nervous."

"So, perhaps, a better analogy would be…that you're as jittery as a novice in her first training session."

Lyndsey snorted her amusement, noting, "That was about the worst thing you could say if you wanted to calm me down."

"Being calm is overrated."

He flipped the lights on and walked inside. "Look around and ask me anything you want," Damien offered as he drew the curtains closed against the darkness outside. "If at any time you become uncomfortable…well more than you are now, just tell me and I'll walk you back to the farmhouse. No harm, no foul. Tonight, is just about getting all your BDSM questions answered."

Her mood lost some of its ebullience, deflating like the slow leak from a balloon. Lyndsey ignored the disappointment his assurances brought because, she told herself, she didn't really want to go any farther than that and because she wasn't a real submissive even if she found it somewhat titillating.

*But not really*, she declared silently.

"What's that!" she asked, sidling over to a strange saddle-like pillow thing mounted on a sturdy sawhorse. An obscenely huge dildo stuck up in the middle drawing her curious fingers forward, but she didn't actually touch it.

"You go right for the good stuff." Amusement laced his tone. "That is the world-famous sex machine, the Sybian. It can be used as a reward or punishment or even a test."

Lyndsey doubted it could work that well, and the doubt must have shown on her face.

"Think jet engine as vibrator." His eyebrows raised in mischief, and he nodded to it with his head. "Take a closer look."

Lyndsey circled the piece. It was then that she noticed steel rings set in the platform in various places, and she could see how a woman could be restrained to it while the device moved beneath her, forcing orgasm after orgasm. Excitement, like a bolt of electric lust, shot through her at the possibility that Damien might force her to climax that way.

Almost as quickly, the erotic adrenaline faded away. She forced her sagging shoulders and sad face into some semblance of "it's no big deal." Lyndsey knew he'd eventually find out her dismal secret—that she didn't have the capacity for earth-shattering climaxes or even halfway decent ones. She wasn't unresponsive, but that kind of total uninhibited passion just wasn't in her. Would Damien quickly become, as her previous boyfriends had, disappointed and then bored with her lackluster sexuality?

Turning decisively, Lyndsey covered her frustration with pretended enthusiasm. She rushed to another piece of furniture. "Okay, so I already saw the St. Andrew's Cross in action, but what's this?"

"Such an eager beaver." Damien chuckled. "Do you want to know how I would use it on you?" The wicked excitement in his grin made her flame, both her face and more private places he couldn't see.

"I didn't say tha-at," she retorted, but neither of them was fooled.

"This is one of my favorite ways to play. I've fantasized about putting you on it." He placed a hand on the giant human-sized wheel attached upright to a sturdy base, and gently caressed the surface of the smooth metal. "I would watch from the throne over there while you stripped for me, and then I'd secure you to this, spread eagle, like da Vinci's Vitruvian Man."

Lyndsey stared at it, fascinated. She could see the restraint loops, but how was it different from the cross.

Damien went behind it and fiddled with something. Walking back around, he held a remote in his hand. He pressed a button and the wheel slowly rotated.

"Oh my." Lyndsey could see herself, naked and slowly being rotated to hang upside down with her legs spread in a wide V. Besides being completely helpless, the wheel would make it super easy for him to apply kink wherever he wanted.

"The open design is unique. It allows for access to the body from the front or back." He circled the wheel, and she could see him behind the spokes. "If I need to punish you for misbehaving, I would have the choice of paddling your ass or your thighs. Perhaps a sharp crop to the tips of your nipples…if they aren't already in the grip of nipple clamps."

"Nipple clamps!"

"Yes, another toy that can be used for pleasure or punishment."

Wanting to seem more sophisticated than she was, Lyndsey parried with a challenge of sorts. "I'm a type A person, you know. If I do become your sub, I'll be a perfect one, always obeying your every command, and you'll never be able to whip me." She gave him a "so there" look.

Damien laughed. "I really do like you…so much." He moved to stand behind her, so close she could almost feel him. Breathing into her ear, he whispered, "My oh-so-sweet and uninformed novice, what you don't realize is that a master has complete control over his submissive. When you're my sub…and you *will* be mine, you'll experience what that means."

Lyndsey shuddered, not from fear but from that familiar gut reaction she had every single time to his Dom-ness. It turned her on like nothing else ever had. A thought occurred to her. Would the elusive overpowering climax, something she'd only felt a couple times in her life, be as easily roused by him as was her lust? The very thought of it sent dizzying waves of desire flushing through her body, and she swayed.

Damien's hands were suddenly on her, holding her upright. Gently, giving her plenty of freedom to pull away, he eased her back against him. His body was a tower of chiseled muscles and heat. One singular hardness pressed against her buttocks. Lyndsey shuddered against him, and was rewarded by a low groan. She liked knowing she affected him as much as he affected her.

"I don't understand," she probed. "If I always obey you then you can't punish me."

"I doubt very much that you'll be able to rein in your feisty and curious nature enough to maintain perfect obedience." He chuckled, and she felt the rumble of his chest against her back, warming her. "However"—his tone darkened to one of husky lust. "Pain can arouse as well as punish."

Before she could think or react or anything, Damien stepped back and his hand smacked forcefully on her ass.

"Aww!" Lyndsey squawked and lurched away from him. Damien released her and she turned to him. "That…that…" Her breath coming in pants, she couldn't at first speak.

"That was just a taste. A good Dom will be able to tell if it arouses or not, increasing or decreasing sensation as needed. A truly masterful Dom, and I'm the very best, can bring a person to the point of climaxing from just pain, that is if he wants to reward a good sub who always obeys."

Lyndsey lurched again, but toward him this time. Standing there, nose to chest, she tilted her face up to him.

Damien gazed at her mouth. "May I?"

He didn't wait for an answer as he enfolded her loosely in his arms and lowered his face to hers. The kiss was sweet, undemanding. Almost a tease. His lips caressed hers, but he was the perfect gentleman otherwise.

Until he wasn't. Damien deepened the kiss and pulled her against him. His body was solid and hot, and she wanted to rub her body on his. His tongue thrust into her mouth. She opened wide in welcome, wanting him inside her everywhere. She was enveloped in him—his heat, scent, taste, and his touch filled her senses, intoxicating her, making her dizzy with desire. Lyndsey moaned into his mouth, wanting more.

When he pulled away, Lyndsey could see that he looked as dazed as she felt. And as hungry. "I know that I said just talking, but..." He led her by the hand to the massive bed and stopped before it.

"I want to show you what it means to be my submissive. But for this night, only pleasure, not pain. May I, Lyndsey?" He said her name like a prayer. "Let me show you what we can be together." Even though Damien released her hands and stepped back, his eyes willed her to yield to him.

It was what she wanted too.

"Yes," Lyndsey whispered. She stared up at him and without conscious thought gave him the respect he deserved. "Sir."

"You honor me." His quietly reverent tone as much as his words told her how deeply her response moved him.

"What should I do, Sir." Her desire to please him made her suddenly shy and unsure how to proceed.

"Nothing. I'll do it all."

"Oh." That wasn't what she'd expected.

Damien stepped back from her. His eyes trailed down her body. "So beautiful." He circled her, ordering, "Just stand still," when Lyndsey started to turn with him. "I really mean this. You have no responsibilities, nothing you need to do or prove. I just want you to enjoy us, together. Our first time."

Lyndsey believed Damien truly meant everything he said, and she relaxed, exhaling the air trapped in her lungs. Unencumbered at last, she could now bask in the hungry adoration that shined in Damien's eyes. She was, at least for this one night, his goddess, deserving of all the pleasure in the world. Weightless and unfettered and wholly open to him and his desires. It was a novel sensation, having always felt inadequate in the past, previous lovers having always found fault in her. She, too, had always assumed she was too blame.

*Not tonight!*

Tonight, she would not hold back. Tonight, she'd give up something much more important than her hymen. She would give up her inhibitions and finally float free. A sensual virgin no more.

Damien circled her again and stopped to stand behind her. His lips gently caressed her neck with barely-there kisses, while his hands slowly dragged her dress upwards, gathering and bunching it. She started to help him.

"No, do nothing unless I tell you. Unless you really want that spanking." But she could hear the teasing in his tone.

He pulled the dress over her head. His fingers grazed her skin as he undid the clasp on her bra and slowly dragged it over her shoulders, before dropping it at her feet. Damien hooked his fingers in her panties and dragged them down until they joined the pile on the floor. Only then, did he start moving slowly around her to face her again.

Sudden realization hit—she was about to stand before him fully naked.

Lyndsey shivered, her entire body trembling and her nipples peaking. Not from cold, but stirred by anticipation.

Then Damien was there in front of her, leering at her body. Everywhere his devouring gaze brushed felt like tiny feathers teasing her skin.

Lyndsey moaned, lust hitting her in rolling waves of need. And still he did nothing but stare.

"So…incredibly…beautiful." Wonder making his timbre soft.

"So…fucking…hot." Desire making him rough.

He grabbed her, pulling her toward him. His lips claimed her in a demanding kiss that branded Lyndsey, making her his.

She was his. Lyndsey felt it to her bones, amazed that she could feel such strong connection to this man she had barely begun to know.

His strong arms swept her from the ground, and in moments she was placed with care in the center of the giant bed.

"Do you trust me?" he asked, leaning over her.

Lyndsey gazed up at him, the feeling of connection, of being with the right person, astoundingly strong.

"Yes, Sir." She was proud of the self-possession and confidence in her voice.

"Your safe word is Burgundy, for this place where I first met you."

That was all he said, before he got to work. He grasped an ankle and secured it to the metal bedframe. And another. Within minutes, she was spread-eagled on the bed, pulled tight. She watched him, feeling helpless, needy even, and realized she liked it.

Damien looked magnificent. Confident. Self-assured. Sexy Leader Guy was back, but this time his cocky arrogant grin was just for her.

From a nightstand, he pulled out a blindfold and placed it around her face. The abrupt darkness was disconcerting. Not knowing what he was about to do made her uneasy. Her mouth opened to object.

*Trust.*

He'd asked her to trust him.

If she actually went through with all of it. If she became his sub, granting him the right to do whatever he wanted to her and her body, she would face this test over and over. Each trial taking her one step closer to true submission and to becoming his in the way that he wanted and needed.

Lyndsey swallowed her reservations and shut her mouth. Then she moaned. Loudly. And pulled on her restraints.

Something tantalizingly soft had brushed across her breasts, followed immediately by a scratchy something, opposing impressions lighting fires across her skin. Over and over, he repeated the process of half bliss, half torment, as he played over her body. Her belly. Her inner thighs. The soles of her feet, the tickling making her jerk but unable to pull away. And, finally, her pussy, the bliss making her arch for more.

The shocking torment, making her cry out. "*Ohhh,*" a louder moan wrenched from her when she felt a new impression. Sharp, almost stinging pricks rolled across her thigh. It circled her mons and traveled up her belly, ever closer to her now highly sensitized tits.

"Ouch." Sharp, quick, pricks rolled over a breast and tightly peaked nipple.

*No more!* Lyndsey shut her mouth firmly against giving him an order, but the safe word hovered in her mind. The barely-there sting was already fading, but she knew he wouldn't stop at tormenting one breast. She panted and tensed, anticipating what was coming.

This time, Lyndsey clenched her mouth tightly, trapping the moan in the back of her throat in a guttural sound so intense her entire body shuddered.

Her besieged nipple was sucked into a hot wet cavern and nothing had ever felt so good. Alternately soothing and tormenting the tight bud, his tongue laved and his teeth nibbled. Lyndsey suddenly understood what he meant about pleasure through pain. These heights could not be reached without the contrasting lows.

Without thought, she urged, "More."

Damien shifted to her other breast, hovering over it. "Subs who make demands are left tied up and unsatisfied."

Lyndsey gasped in disbelief. *No!* But this time she managed to keep her edict silent.

But not her reactions. "Ouch." Damien had bit her tit sharply.

"This one time only, your wish is my command. I'll give you more." Lyndsey could hear the playful happiness in his voice, and it thrilled her that he was enjoying this so much too.

"I'm not going to speak again," he added, hovering over her breast. "But I want you to know you're safe with me. When I'm done playing, when I think you're ready, I'll remove the blindfold so you can watch me put on a rubber. Then I'm going to take you. Hard."

Pure blazing lust shot through Lyndsey like a lightning bolt. She moaned and squirmed and wanted to tell him she was ready now. But he'd warned her against giving orders, so she locked her lips tight.

"If you don't want that, tell me now," he ordered.

Lyndsey already knew the answer, but he hadn't asked for anything but her refusal, so she kept her mouth shut and waited. Her mind and entire body on high alert.

"Okay. Let's begin."

*Begin?* Hadn't he already turned her into a bundle of igniting fiery nerves.

Damien left her for a moment, and when he returned he began again, but with more toys. Sharp little flicks of something. Soothing sweeps of feathers. Electric vibrations on her pussy. Damien didn't let up for a moment, and Lyndsey was uncontrollably swept away on myriad sensations, her body and mind no longer hers to command.

Her skin was alive, almost a separate being from herself. It wanted more, more, more. More of everything he was doing to her.

Her mouth sought him, kissing him eagerly whenever his face drew near. Her hands pulled at the restraints and clenched uselessly at the air, wanting to touch him, the helplessness its own eroticism. Her breasts arched into whatever torture or bliss he offered. Always too brief. Just short of total titillation. And worst, her clit ached for more, her core clenching on nothing.

Damien's hands, his toys, and his skill were driving her out of her mind. More times than she could count, Lyndsey opened her mouth to make demands, barely remembering his warning, but still he kept playing, kept pushing her body to accept more arousal, until she thought she couldn't take a single touch more.

Never before in her life had Lyndsey endured such overwhelming, all-consuming lust. Damien had awakened her body, making her come alive and on fire. Burning bright in a way she hadn't known she could experience. No one had ever taken the time to show her what she was capable of. This was Damien's gift to her. It added a frosting of warm delight to the tormenting pleasure.

Still he relentlessly worked her need even higher for what seemed like hours. Repeatedly, he took her to the edge, so close she could see the white-hot climax just out of reach, and then he'd ease back, forcing whimpers of need from her. He soothed and kissed away her agony, calming her, only to start anew rebuilding the fires that consumed her, until Lyndsey was moaning and continuously thrashing about sightless on the large bed, pulling on her restraints. Mindless. Boneless. Floating.

Abruptly her mask was pulled away and she blinked in the dim light. Damien was kneeling over her, naked and strong. He had secured a condom as covertly as he'd undressed. He held it up for her to see, before expertly rolling it down his thick shaft.

Lyndsey raised her head. He was huge. She wanted to see more, see all of him, but after hours of play, Damien was now in a hurry. Poised at her entrance in seconds, he looked up at her. Waiting. Wanting again her permission.

She raised her pelvis to meet him, and with a groan of sheer pleasure, Damien seated himself all the way inside her. Lyndsey felt the full surge of him and completion finally drew near.

But Damien retreated, pulling nearly all the way out, holding himself momentarily aloft. "So wet," he muttered through clenched teeth.

She raised her pelvis again in offering, wanting him back, and he grinned down at her. "Sweet novice, you're going to learn a great deal about delayed gratification."

Lyndsey suddenly hated the restraints. She growled and bucked her pelvis forcefully, and he laughed.

"Yes, my soon-to-be trainee, I'm going to tease the livin' daylights out of you."

Lyndsey screeched in frustration.

"But not tonight," he pronounced, laughing boyishly.

He thrust urgently back inside her, and this time he didn't retreat. Damien, a.k.a. Master Edge, was done edging her.

Holding himself up on his elbows, he powered into her, over and over. So big he filled her completely, the intense push and pull utterly delicious. And Lyndsey met his every thrust with nearly equal force. She all but fainted from the intense friction. The pleasure so overwhelming, she could cry big tears, and perhaps she did. There was wetness on her cheeks.

"You're incredibly sexy," Damien exclaimed, pounding ever faster within her.

"You are too," she cried, bucking madly to meet each pulse, always needing more.

He claimed her mouth, and she opened to him, opened with everything she had, and he groaned into her. Lyndsey ceased being herself in that moment. Almost as if she were flying free outside her body, she became sex and cried out joyfully.

The desire he'd built so skillfully within her carried her ever higher toward something heretofore always out of reach. And then it wasn't.

Lyndsey exploded into a million brilliant shards of white-hot ecstasy. The feeling beyond pleasure. Beyond herself. And for a wonderful moment she lived in it, Damien using his skill to keep her poised there in the bright mindless euphoria.

Damien cried out, juddering one last time, and though barely conscious, she knew that he'd joined her in bliss, and she raised her pelvis one last time to tightly hold him there with her, their special connection finally complete.

Understanding of where she was slowly returned to her and she opened her eyes. Damien smiled down at her. "That was wonderful," he murmured, and pecked a quick kiss on her lips.

"I agree."

"Let me get you out of these." He pulled out of her, and Lyndsey instantly regretted the loss.

Within minutes, Damien had the restraints off and had her tucked under a warm blanket. After bringing her a glass of cool water, he turned off the lights and joined her under the covers to snuggle next to her.

"Thank you," he murmured in her ear, sounding half asleep. Soon he went under, his arm wrapped securely around her.

As soothing sleep began to overtake her, Lyndsey marveled at what they'd just done and at the knowledge that she wasn't frigid. Damien had shown her everything she was capable of, and she'd experienced the kind of deep satisfying orgasm that had always eluded her in the past.

Lyndsey snorted. "If this is what it means to be a sub, I'm all in."

"Mmm…wha…"

"Shh, it's nothing," Lyndsey whispered, remaining quiet until she was sure he was all the way out. No point in letting him win that easily, she thought, grinning and naughty.

Abruptly, Lyndsey wondered what her friends would say if they knew where she was and what she'd just done. With effort, she pushed the unsettling thought away. She was an adult, right? Could make her own choices. Still it didn't seem likely she would ever tell them or anyone...and especially not her parents. The idea of keeping secrets from those close to her didn't sit well, and sleep wouldn't come.

When sheep didn't work, Lyndsey tried focusing on the good things.

Damien was nice.

Considerate.

Handsome.

A good cook. Wouldn't her mom love that! Especially since Lyndsey couldn't even boil an egg.

And there was more...but at last her mind was starting to slow.

The list of good things could wait. Then she stopped thinking at all and finally slept.

# Chapter 9

---

*~ achy but feeling good*

Full consciousness came slowly. In the twinkle of morning light and the chirp of a bird. In the growing awareness that she wasn't in her own bed, and in the slow realization of where she really was. *The Burgundy Rose.*

Eyes still closed, Lyndsey smiled, remembering the wondrous pleasure of the night before, her well-used body both tingly and achy. But it was the abrupt awareness that she was alone in the bed that jerked her fully awake.

Lyndsey sat up clutching the blanket to her chest and looked around.

She was definitely alone.

The curtains were pulled apart just enough to shine a little light into the empty building. There was a note on the pillow next to her.

*Dear Lyndsey,*

*I didn't want to wake you, so slipped out quietly. As we discussed, you should come over to the bistro whenever you're up and I'll make you the world's best omelet. But*

*take your time. There's bubble bath for the tub if you*
*want. Last night was A M A Z I N G, just like you.*
*See you soon.*

*Your personal chef in public, and*
*soon-to-be master in private (I hope),*

*Damien*

Lyndsey giggled. "I like the sound of that...my very own personal chef." Yes, her mom would approve, even if she didn't approve of the other part.

A bath would be great to ease her aches and pains, and Lyndsey climbed out of bed. She donned the plush robe she found draped over the large claw-foot tub that stood alone in the dungeon, near but not in the bathroom. Strange, that, but not nearly as weird as the fact that a giant glass-walled shower was also out in the space along the wall. No privacy at all, but maybe that was the point.

While the bathtub filled, she puttered about, fingering the various lewd implements and kinky equipment. Lyndsey gathered the used items strewn about the floor. Toys, Damien had called them. Looking at the assortment in her hands, they looked foreign and strange. No longer filled with lust, it now struck Lyndsey as odd that she'd let this man, no matter how much she liked him, do all this stuff to her while she was helplessly tied up and blindfolded. At least now she knew what Damien had used on her—something made of strips of soft rabbit fur, a metal wheelie-thing with spikes, a horse crop, and some kind of glove with sort-of sandpaper on it. In the light of day, the "toys" looked...sordid.

She put them out of sight in a hamper, marked "Used Toys."

Leaving those thoughts behind, Lyndsey walked to the tub and removed her robe. She lowered herself into the warm bubble bath, feeling like a queen on Sunday. "Mm." She could get used to this lifestyle.

Relaxing back, head resting against the tub's rim, she let her eyes roam about, no destination in mind, just taking it all in. Such a lot of bizarre, expensive equipment. All of it was über luxurious and designed for one thing—hedonistic pleasure. Spying the cage hanging from the ceiling, she looked again with narrowed eyes. More specifically, most of it was about restraining human beings, turning them into helpless recipients of whatever depraved delights their jailor could devise.

Lyndsey smiled, remembering her incredible orgasm brought about by Damien's devious treatment of her, but that was only part of it. The cages, the St. Andrew's Cross, even the bed, all of it could be used to brutally punish people, inflict pain with or without their consent. Some of it looked vicious. Cruel even.

*What am I getting myself into?*

The unbidden prompt sent her upright, water sloshing out of the tub. Her eyes swept the space again, seeing it differently. BDSM wasn't as exciting and special this morning. Instead, kink seemed sordid and a little vulgar, the idea of servicing men naked on one's knees, not daring but degrading.

And, how could she keep something as monumentally huge as becoming a sex slave a secret? Well maybe from her parents residing in Santa Barbara she could manage it, but what about her closest friends? Wouldn't Beth notice something?

Notice that Lyndsey acted weirdly around Damien or, remembering the bruises and welts some of the subs had sported, possibly see the physical marks of slave training on her body?

Lyndsey lifted her arms out of the water and brushed off the bubbles. Turning them this way and that, she didn't see any marks…yet. A careful check revealed nothing on the rest of her, except very red skin on her sore nipples.

"That's a relief."

She settled back into the soothing bubbles, but her mind was anything but soothed. All the hedonism and happiness and hope of last night had vanished. She liked Damien well enough. "He's a great guy," she declared loudly to the empty room. It was just what came with him that was the problem. Explicitly, her submission to him.

Even if she really was, as Damien believed, a true submissive—and her reaction today to everything in the dungeon made her doubt it—how could she go through with it all? Allow herself to be trained to obediently serve him, even against her own wishes. Lower herself so thoroughly that she'd willingly debase herself in whatever demeaning manner he commanded. Even allow him the right to chastise her, a grown adult, with spankings, pain, or other humiliating penalties.

Then again, if she didn't have these proclivities, why did the mere thought of kneeling naked in front of Damien make her yearn? There was no denying that she got turned-on every single time he even playfully threatened to take her over his knee. And he knew it.

Maybe Damien was right, and she was this so-called "natural" submissive, but there didn't seem to be anything natural or normal about it in the light of day. Twenty years of hearing what was right and good, and what was wrong and evil, couldn't be tuned out and turned off that easily. And who was to say her parents were wrong in their conservative beliefs? The people here in this room called it kink and themselves kinksters. Sure it sounded trendy, but that didn't make it right.

*What's wrong with me that I would even consider exploring this?*

Lyndsey debated it silently until the water grew cold. Unsure what to do, she dressed and left the dungeon, trudging up to the farmhouse. Perhaps it would be best to pack up and leave straightaway. Make a clean break. However, the thought of not seeing Damien again hurt, made her heart ache. The pain of it seemed far worse than any cropping could ever sting.

Lyndsey snorted, realizing the truth of it.

*I want the cropping.*

For a moment, hope flared—maybe Damien could try a lesser version, a sort of BDSM-lite—but the optimism didn't last long. He'd been honest with her from the beginning. Damien was also Master Edge, a Dom who wasn't going to change. It was wrong of her to expect it when he'd been very clear about what he needed. In the end, Lyndsey came to a brutal conclusion—she wasn't afraid of being his sub, even admitted to craving it, there was just no way she could reconcile having such a relationship apart from the rest of her daily life.

Entering the farmhouse, she smelled the remains of breakfast and her stomach grumbled. Damien had wanted her to join him at the restaurant, but she just couldn't face him right now. Everything was too unsettled, and he might try to sway her to his side. She went into the dining room and saw the owner cleaning up.

"I guess I missed breakfast." Lyndsey didn't even know what time it was, having left her cellphone in the guestroom upstairs.

"Yes, I'm sorry. It's from eight to ten on the weekends, but, hey, why don't you come into the kitchen, and I can easily whip up some fresh scrambled eggs. And there's some leftover sausage I can reheat."

"If it's not too much trouble."

Catriona smiled and said, "None at all for a friend of Damien's."

Within minutes, Lyndsey was digging into steaming food and hot coffee and thanking Cat between mouthfuls.

Catriona joined her at the kitchen table with her own mug. "I don't have any new guests today, so I can relax a little."

"This place is really nice." Lyndsey had a thousand questions, wondering how this sweet young woman had come to own a B&B or more to the point, a clandestine wine-house dungeon.

"Look, I'm glad we have a moment alone," Cat said, setting her mug down. "I want to apologize for how you discovered The Burgundy Rose. None of my regular guests were supposed to be exposed to the seminar, but I'm going to put up a gate and that should help."

"No, it was my fault. I went for a walk late at night."

"And there was no reason you shouldn't have." She smiled at Lyndsey, seeming to weigh her next words. "I guess it worked out all right. You and Damien, I mean."

"He's a great guy." Lyndsey didn't know what else to say.

"I know that you spent last night in the wine house, and he's rented it for the entire weekend. If you want, you can check out of the B&B and move your things there. I don't feel right charging for a room you're not using."

"Oh. I...ah." Lyndsey took a big gulp of her coffee, but for once it didn't work as a stall. She choked and sputtered for several minutes. "Sorry," she gasped.

"Went down the wrong pipe?"

Lyndsey nodded. Finally able to catch her breath, she said, "That doesn't seem right. I reserved the room for the whole weekend, and you could have had other guests. Anyway, I'm thinking of heading home today."

"Oh? Damien said you'd be here through Sunday. Is everything okay?"

The moment stretched, while Lyndsey contemplated the woman. She needed to talk to someone and there certainly wasn't anyone back home that would understand.

"It's, well..." Lyndsey lowered her voice to a whisper. "Can I ask you about...you know, the dungeon and stuff?" Cat looked a little taken aback, and Lyndsey hastily added, "I mean it's totally fine if you don't want to."

"No, I don't mind, and if there's something I can't or shouldn't answer, I'll tell you."

Lyndsey took a deep breath and let it all out. "It's not that I judge the people I saw in there at the seminar or even Damien and what he does. They're all consenting adults and what they do is their business, but I was raised differently. My parents are devoutly religious and would never understand...that." She gestured in the general vicinity of the wine house. "It's not how I was raised, either."

Cat's eyebrow rose on hearing her last statement. "I can tell you about BDSM and why I like it, but this is a very personal thing. Each person comes to the lifestyle for their own reasons. If you're emotionally healthy...you are, aren't you?"

Lyndsey nodded. "I think so."

"Then how you choose to interact with the people you love is your business. Have you ever heard of SSC?"

Lyndsey shook her head, and Cat explained, "It stands for Safe, Sane, and Consensual. It means that safety is the number-one priority in all BDSM play, and that the participants are sane and give their legal consent. I demand this rule be followed in my dungeon, and it's what I live by too."

"Are you..." Lyndsey paused, thinking she was heading into private territory. "I am curious whether you're a Dom or a sub?"

Cat gave her a smile that glowed, like the sun on a bright spring morning. "I'm a true blue submissive. Not twenty-four-seven, meaning all the time, but when I'm alone in the dungeon with my man, that's what fulfills me, both sexually and emotionally." She shined with inner pleasure and pride.

"And you're...um...perfectly okay with that? I mean, don't you ever want to say no or get angry when your Dom wants something you don't want to do?"

Cat reached over and squeezed her hand. "Well, first, you have to understand that it's a power exchange."

"Yeah, Damien mentioned that."

"What that means is not only do I give him the power, but I get to set how much or how wide that is...and it doesn't have to be static. We're no different than anyone else. Our needs can change over time and so we negotiate when we need a change in our relationship."

"Wow. So really, just like a normal couple." Lyndsey saw a quick grimace flash across Cat's face. "I mean, of course, you're normal, but…"

"The second point is that just like "normal" couples,"— Cat winked at her—"we fight sometimes, but that doesn't mean that our modus operandi is wrong. We argue, negotiate, and work it out, like anyone else."

"Oh, of course. I'm just conflicted. I believe in equality of the sexes but…" Lyndsey couldn't keep the private grin from her face. "Well, let's just say, that Master Edge knows his business."

"Good. I'm glad to hear that he treated you right." She rose from the table. "Now I'd better get the dishes done so I can return all those phone calls I ignored in the rush of breakfast." Cat indicated the blinking light on her old-fashioned answering machine. "I'm old school when it comes to my tech, but I find it easier to deal with." She walked over and switched the machine off and immediately the landline rang.

Cat answered it and then turned back to her, a surprised look on her face. "It's for you, a Carla Thompson."

Lyndsey walked over and took the receiver from her. "Hello."

"Hi Lynd, just wanted to see if you're okay. Beth's worried because she's been calling since yesterday evening and you haven't answered or even texted. She's convinced that you've crashed and died on the freeway, so I told her I'd find a way to reach you."

"Oh, I'm sorry. I…" Lyndsey couldn't say she'd spent the night in a dungeon tied to a bed. "Sorry, I must have turned off the ringer. But I'm fine and had a lovely dinner last night with Chef Damien."

"Ooo! You'll have to give us more juicy details than that."

"Later okay. Places to go, stuff to do. Yay know."

"Okay, okay. Just glad to hear you're not dead." Carla laughed at her own humor. "Oh, by the way, Trish wants to know if you got a peek inside the dungeon. I can't see what she finds so fascinating about it. No accounting for taste, but anyway I'm relaying her question."

"I…um." She looked at Cat for guidance but, of course, the woman, busy loading the dishwasher, couldn't hear the conversation. It went against Lyndsey's upbringing to lie, so she made a joke of it. "Tell Trish I'll try to snap some photos…*Not!* Thanks for calling and caring."

Carla wished her a safe trip home and hung up.

"Thanks again for breakfast," she told Cat, about to head upstairs. Lyndsey now understood the power dynamics a little better but was still struggling to decide if she should pursue things with Damien.

Cat wiped her hands on her apron. "So, what are you going to do? Head home or—"

The door from the back patio burst open, and Damien barged in.

"Where the fuck have you been?" He marched up to Lyndsey looking angry as hell.

"I…um…why are you so angry?"

"I've been trying to reach you for hours when you didn't show for breakfast. I've left messages on your cell phone and here at the farmhouse."

Lyndsey was elated that Damien had missed her and relieved when his irate gaze swiveled to Cat. "Why the fuck didn't you answer the phone? You run a business, or so I thought."

Cat didn't look the least perturbed, calmly pouring herself another cup of coffee. "I often let calls go to my machine during breakfast or I'd never get food on the table." She tipped her head in a nod of farewell and left them alone in the kitchen.

Damien swung back to face Lyndsey, his angry visage softening. "I was worried about you. Thought maybe you got lost or hurt or something else bad." He came closer and reached for her hand. Lyndsey let him hold it, but didn't draw closer.

"I'm a grown woman. I can take care of myself."

"I know." He snorted. His eyes, shining with a decidedly naughty glint, flicked in the general direction of the wine house. "Believe me, I do know that. But in the three weeks of our long-distance relationship, there wasn't one single time, not once, that you didn't immediately respond back to me, even if it was just to text that you were busy."

"I'm sorry about that. It was a mistake. I left my cell in the farmhouse and forgot about it."

"Okay, so why didn't you come to the bistro? I was expecting you, and when you didn't show, I closed it down early to drive out here. I don't think the owners are going to be too pleased about that."

"I'm really very sorry." Lyndsey felt awful now, and it was only going to get worse. "The truth is, well, I'm having doubts about…you know." She too flicked her eyes toward the dungeon.

"Come with me. We're going to talk."

It wasn't a request, the full weight of his control-freak Dom-ness saturated every syllable. He'd turned toward the outside door, tugging her along, not considering for a second whether her assent was necessary.

Lyndsey resisted. "I don't want to go in there."

That seemed to flummox him and he stopped. Damien snorted again, his hand brushing down the back of his head as he stared at her in concentration. After a moment, he said, "It's too public here, but there's a bench outside the wine house. Why don't we go there."

"Okay."

She let him tug her along this time. They walked the short distance in silence, but out of the corner of her eye she saw him glance repeatedly at her. The bench was just past the hedge, affording some privacy. He waited until she sat, then joined her.

"Start again," he ordered. "Tell me what's wrong, and be specific."

Lyndsey kept her face neutral, but inside she smiled. Damien's dominance, his need to control, was more prominent than ever when he was upset, and she could tell that he was by the mix of urgency and longing in his expression.

His hand started tapping on his thigh, and he leaned in closer. "Well?"

"I'm sorry," she said.

"Yes, you've said that. Three times."

"It's hard to explain."

"Okay, tell me this, didn't you like what we did last night?" Now he looked uneasy. "I mean, I thought you liked it."

"Oh, Damien!" She scooted closer. "Yes, you know I did. It was *amazing*. What you did was like a gift to me." She looked down at her lap. "I'm embarrassed to tell you but I…um…I've never had that before."

"Sex?" Doubt registered in his tone and mien.

"No," she laughed. "I mean, I've never…" Her face heated and her pulse raced. It was so humiliating to admit. Damien reached out and squeezed her hand, reassuringly.

"I don't think I've ever had an orgasm before. I mean, it seemed like I had. However, last night was something altogether different, a thousand times more. Better. Like I said, amazing."

He puffed up at her praise, a satisfied smirk leaking past his self-control. "So what's the problem?"

"This is really hard because I really like you, and I think you like me too."

He nodded.

"It's just that, while I liked the sex, the whole kink thing is a problem."

He opened his mouth to respond, but she rushed forward wanting to get it all out there. "First, I don't think I'm a submissive, no matter what you say. I believe in equality of the sexes."

He looked like he wanted to object, but she held up her hand. "Okay, I admit. I do like the sex and the role playing, I guess. But how can I explore this new side of myself and still be me. My family and I are close, even if our politics are different. They'd never understand how I could become a submissive. They wouldn't understand any of it, and neither would my friends. So, I was thinking it would be better if I ended this now. Not get in too deep."

His eyes narrowed. "Were you just going to leave?"

Lyndsey blushed again, realizing how close to that she'd come.

He stared at her, both hurt and anger flaring in his eyes.

Unable to stand the censure she saw there, she lurched to her feet and paced, gaze downcast. She mumbled, "I admit that I considered it. Seemed like it might be easier."

"For who?"

"Oh, Damien," she wailed, turning back to him. "I've handled this all so badly, but it doesn't change anything. I'm afraid that if I pursue this it will cause so many problems in my personal life, maybe even my career. And what in the flying fuck will my parents think if they find out?"

Damien rose too and walked to her. "You've thrown out a lot of concerns, but I think the biggest obstacle for you is about privacy. It's all brand new and raw, I get that, and you worry what those close to you will think. That they'll reject you. I can see that this is a deal-breaker for you."

She nodded. "I'm glad you get it. Makes it easier." Conflicting emotion washed through her, equal parts relief that he understood and remorse that she was about to lose her newest friend. Lyndsey already felt so close to him, so utterly simpatico, that she wondered if she'd ever feel that again for someone else.

"However, I ask you, how will they ever know unless you tell them?" His tone now stronger, Damien sounded again like Sexy Leader Guy. "What we do in the bedroom is between you and me. Whether you're on your knees submissively or I am. Ha!" Damien chortled abruptly, like a single thunderclap. "That's one place you'll never find me. Regardless, how we fuck is private. Do you post on social media about your latest orgasm?"

"Of course not."

"Do your friends?"

"No, but—"

"Sex is private. Our business and no one else's. As for me being a Dom and you a sub, it's completely our decision how secret we decide to keep it. I'm not ashamed of my enjoyment of kink, but I work at a local business and can't risk some idiot dissing the place in a review because of how I like to make love."

"Okay, I get it. It's our business. But I've never been into kink."

"Last night you were."

Lyndsey blushed yet again, unable to deny it. "Well it's not who I am, really. I believe in equality. I will never become your slave." She stared out at the grapevines, this place having held so much promise, would be missed nearly as much as the man next to her.

His hand on her face drew her back to him. "I think, maybe, that you haven't really heard what I've said about my needs or perhaps you don't believe me, so I'll say it again. I don't want, have never wanted, a 24/7 slave. What I do need is to dominate sexually. I can't see myself changing, but outside of that you would always be my full and equal partner. It's up to you, because whoever shares my life has to accept what I am." He grasped her hands, holding them firmly, yet loose enough that she could pull away if she wanted.

He looked hopeful and scared at the same time. "I'll understand if you still want to leave, but I wish you would stay."

The way he looked at her, so tenderly, made Lyndsey wanted to stay right there with him forever. He had lessened, if not eliminated, her fears, and she had never before shied away from seeking what she truly wanted.

She realized that it was do or die time, admit the truth or go home.

And the truth was, she wanted Damien.

And she also wanted Master Edge.

Was she strong enough to go for it even with the uncertainties that came with him?

She threw out a foray. "I really like you, Damien. Very much."

"And I care about you too. Very much." He leaned close and nuzzled her nose as he had done the night before. "Tell me," he whispered, willing her with his eyes to maintain their connection. "What does your gut say…what do you want to do right now, this very instant?"

For the fourth time that afternoon, Lyndsey, who rarely blushed, turned bright, flaming, scarlet red. But she'd made her decision and wouldn't back down.

"I want to go inside The Burgundy Rose, and I want more, much more, of what we did last night."

"Really?" Damien laughed boyishly, looking happy and eager.

Quickly, before doubts could assail her, she exclaimed, "Yes. Right now."

Cocking his elbow, he offered his arm to her. "I stand corrected. I might have said last night that I wouldn't take orders from you, but, once again…" He waggled his elbow, and she took his arm. "Once again, your wish is my command."

# Chapter 10

---

*~ go big or go home*

But Damien paused when they reached the locked wine house. "Lyndsey, we can take it slow or maybe just go out to dinner."

She shook her head.

"Or we can repeat last night. Or…we can move forward exploring our needs and each other. As I said before, it's all up to you. You have the real power."

Excitement skittered down her back. It was clear by the way he'd emphasized the last option, that he wanted more kink. Probably wanted her sexual submission in ways she couldn't imagine, and that very thought made her breasts feel heavy and her pelvis tighten. It told her what she desired even if it scared her at the same time.

"Let's move forward." She sounded breathy, feminine, even to her own ears.

"You honor me with your trust. That you're offering me the power to guide you inside these walls is a gift. I promise to cherish it and cherish you, putting your needs above mine."

Lyndsey was shaken by how meaningful his pledge sounded. His deep commitment gave her the courage to ask for what she'd been too afraid to even admit to herself that she needed.

"I think that I would like you to train me to be your submissive. I want it all, no half steps."

Now it was Damien who looked stunned. "Are you sure?"

"Yes, completely, with my whole heart. Let's start this now."

Her declaration pleased him greatly, she could see that, but he spoke in a serious tone. "I want you to know that you'll always have a safe word, an out. That's my promise. But at the same time, once you enter, you become *mine*, to train as I see fit. If we're to do this, I must become your master and you must accept that before entering. Think of stepping through this door as entering an alternate universe with new rules that are set in stone for eternity. There will be no changing them, not with me, not unless I change them. Outside, I will always treat you like an equal. Think of you as my partner in all decisions, but there is one more thing."

Lyndsey had trembled at every provoking assertion he made. "Yes. What else?" Her voice held less strength now.

"While you and I are equals out here,"—he gestured broadly to the space around them—"our behavior toward each other can't help but affect our D/s relationship inside with all the resulting ramifications. Do you understand?"

She didn't really. However, Lyndsey nodded, thinking she'd figure it out later.

Damien unlocked the door and stepped to the side. He was waiting for her to take the first step, *literally*.

Lyndsey nodded once and pushed the door open. She stepped through the portal already shaking with nerve-racking anticipation. She moved to her old spot against the wall, waiting for instructions, watching him as he shut the door.

He turned to face her, wearing a huge eager grin. Perhaps too eager.

But then, his demeanor started to alter. Fascinated, she watched Damien transform. Strolling casually in a large circle, he seemed to take over the large space and everything in it, changing before her eyes, becoming once again the man who had first enthralled her. Sexy Leader Guy.

He studied each piece of equipment, concentrating while flicking glances her way. She wondered what would happen if she told him her preference.

*No*, she silently corrected, realizing her first mistake. *He is my master in here.*

He faced her and changed yet again. His stance relaxed a little, seemed to lose some of that leadership aura. It was replaced with something else, she couldn't quite define. He studied her, observing her from this angle and that. It was difficult to stand still under the spotlight of his intense regard. She wanted to squirm, to twitch. To call him out, and ask him what he was thinking and what he planned to do to her.

Damien met her gaze, and Lyndsey gasped, recognizing the new facet radiating from his impassioned eyes—pride of ownership. He was a powerful, imposing ruler, but one who wanted only one subject.

Her.

He was her master now.

He was Master Edge triumphantly planning the training of his personal thrall.

Damien grinned at her, giving her a glimpse of just how wicked were his thoughts. She quivered, tingles dancing excitedly through her body. She would never understand how just a look from him could turn her into molten, lustful mush, but her body was evidence it was true. Lyndsey moaned aloud, and didn't try to cover it. He was going to ferret out her sexual secrets anyway, so why try to hide.

He gave her a nod, almost a salute, before walking to the magnificent, wing-back chair that stood on a small platform. He jumped up the two steps and settled himself comfortably on the luxurious, red-leather seat, leaning back to watch her. She recognized it as the dungeon's throne. Would he expect her to prostrate herself before it?

"Trainee, come here and stand before me."

Lyndsey hurried over, it being almost a relief to move after standing so still. About two feet from the platform, she stopped and looked up at him.

God! He was magnificent. So dark and dangerous and sexy. His eyes glittered, their black depths, mysterious. A king at his leisure, Damien regarded her with apparent calm, but his look claimed her with such fierce possession, her knees started to bend of their own accord. One lock of his tousled black hair fell across his forehead, the only outward sign of the boyish joy hidden within in him. But it was his raw masculinity that turned her lusciously acquiescent, making her feel weak. Feminine. Needy.

She'd fall down to prostrate herself for him in a heartbeat if he asked.

"We're going to take this slow. You are to tell me the minute something is too much. Do you understand?"

"Yes." Even her tone sounded yielding.

"That's, Yes Sir," he corrected. "Always in the dungeon or bedroom."

"Oh." Lyndsey wasn't sure she'd ever get used to this. Not because she had to call him Sir, but because the rule itself made her belly curl deliciously.

She dropped her gaze and obediently replied, "Yes, Sir."

"Good girl."

Equally unsettling was the flush of pleasure that bloomed within her body at his mild praise.

*Who am I?* The meek and fawning creature standing before Damien was someone she'd never met before.

"Undress for me. Slowly. I want you to seduce me."

A skittering sensation that started between her shoulders, zinged down her spine to her pussy. Lyndsey had guessed this was coming, but now as she reached for her blouse it was so much harder than she'd expected. The obeisant act of performing a striptease for a fully-clothed man, who did nothing more to deserve it than make the request, made her skin crawl hot and cold and shivery. This was so far outside her comfort zone, she might as well be stripping on Times Square.

Damien cleared his throat, jolting her into yanking the top off quickly. His left eyebrow rose, and she read his unspoken assessment: That is not seductive.

Lyndsey dropped her face down to hide her chagrin, but she was too much a Type-A to take that sitting down, or more accurately, standing up. Ignoring the rioting butterflies in her belly, she started to move to seductive music she created in her mind. Swaying, she undid the zipper on her skirt and shimmied

it down over her hips. She hazarded a glance up, and was rewarded by the hungry expression on his face.

Emboldened, Lyndsey pretended she was a star on Broad-
way, a Gypsy Rose Lee stripper for the 21st Century. Grateful
for having selected sexy stilettos over comfort, she strutted in a
circle to show off her skimpy lingerie. After rolling her shoulders
and jiggling her breasts, she undid her bra and dropped it down.

Then she gave him her twerking backside. Undulating her
hips, she pushed her panties down her thighs, until they too slid
to the floor. As she rotated to face him, she scooped up the slip
of satin and tossed it to him.

He snatched her panties from the air. Eyes locked with
hers, Lyndsey gasped when he blatantly sniffed her the fabric.
Giving her a cocky grin, he tucked her underwear into his pants
pocket.

But he wasn't done with her.

"Turn around. Slowly." Only three words, quietly spoken,
but ringing with absolute authority.

Lyndsey obeyed, flushing with excitement. She could feel
Damien's eyes on her everywhere, like a lustful caress, and her
body reacted to him, becoming moist between her thighs.

Rather than embarrassment, she took pride in her new-
found sexual response. She was finally welcoming the erotic
spirit that had hidden within her all along.

"Turn your back to me. Spread your feet two feet apart
and bend over as far as you can, hands to the floor."

"What?" It was obscene, the pose he wanted from her. "I
don't think I can do—"

"Turn your back. Spread your feet. Bend over as far as you
can." There was no change to the tenor of his voice, but she

understood that by saying it twice it was an order to be obeyed. Or else.

With great effort, Lyndsey forced herself to comply until her ass was high and her head hung between her legs. From her upside-down position, she could see Damien on his throne eyeing her ass cheeks and the wet folds underneath. She was utterly exposed, both her pussy and her willingness to debase herself on full view.

"So fucking hot," Damien muttered in a voice husky and hoarse.

A flush of pleasure swept through Lyndsey. Still bent over, she watched him descend the throne.

"Come here," he ordered.

Damien didn't wait for her. Stepping forward, he pulled Lyndsey up and whirled her around. Claiming his new possession, he slammed his lips down on hers. He kissed her passionately, while his hands roamed her body, squeezing, fondling, caressing. Leaving a trail of electric desire wherever he touched, he set Lyndsey afire with dizzying arousal.

She smirked, even as he continued to kiss her. *This subbing thing isn't half bad.*

Without a word, he left her and returned to his place of authority. She could barely tell that he was pleased, so bland and bored did he look sitting on the throne. Only the slightest quirk of his lips gave any outward sign that their monumental kiss had affected him at all, while she could barely stand upright.

"Sweet novice, before we can continue this pleasant training, we must deal with the less agreeable task of discipline."

"What?" She jerked out of her sensual haze to stare at him, wide eyed.

Damien's dark head tilted sidewise, his grin bigger. "Forget the use of Sir at your peril."

Lyndsey huffed. Irritation flared at his highhandedness, but she tamped it down. "What do you mean…*Sir.*" She drawled out the respectful moniker with thinly veiled sarcasm.

While his eyes sparkled, Damien shook his head woefully. "We're going to have such fun. Well, I am anyway."

Lyndsey stamped her foot. Fuming. But she kept her mouth shut.

Damien laughed aloud at her predicament, before re-assuming his severe mien. "As I was saying, before pleasure, must come duty. I know we've talked about this, but I hope you'll grasp the concept somewhat quickly, the better for your behind."

Lyndsey's ass clenched at his innuendo, sending tremors through her body like mini earthquakes.

Trying to appear firm but not hiding his enthusiasm well, Damien continued, "The concept I'm referring to is trust. It's absolutely essential in a D/s relationship. When you didn't show up, I became worried that something was wrong. You made no attempt to let me know you weren't coming. Can you imagine how I felt during those hours?"

"I know, Sir, but that happened outside the dungeon, so it doesn't count."

"That's what I meant by ramifications of our actions throughout our relationship. Your thoughtless behavior had real negative consequences for me. I was extremely concerned, unable to continue working, and possibly lost the restaurant revenue as well, when a simple text would have fixed it."

Abruptly, Lyndsey felt small, and not in a good way. Yes, she'd been dealing with her own worries, but she had acted thoughtlessly.

"I'm very sorry, Sir. I won't do that again."

"That makes me happy to hear, but there's more. You compounded your error by planning to leave me without even a goodbye. Can you imagine how I would have felt? Worse, you didn't trust me enough to share your concerns. We can't have this kind of intense relationship, any kind really, without trust on both sides."

"I see that now. I understand." And Lyndsey meant it. She regretted all of it, now.

"You're a grown adult who's made it clear you desire a very adult liaison, as well as one of equals. Did you act like an adult?"

"Well, no, but—"

"In my world, our world now, misbehavior requires correction. BDSM-style correction. Do you understand and agree there must be consequences?"

Lyndsey trembled. Would it hurt too much to bear?

Her body again betrayed her true feelings, her pussy pulsing deliciously at just the hint of him punishing her ass.

Regardless of her fear or excitement, Lyndsey had to admit that he'd made his case well. She couldn't pretend otherwise. Deciding she'd start this trusting stuff right now, she conceded with a tip of her head.

"Take off your shoes and go to that bench, over there." Damien pointed, and she recognized it as the same piece of furniture he'd nearly spanked her on before. "I promise to be lenient, in part because we don't know your tolerance for pain yet and because you didn't know my rules. But there must always be consequences."

Lyndsey nodded and walked slowly to the bench, the cool air wafting on her naked body reminding her how exposed she was, her bare feet padding on the cold slate tiles reminding her of her reduced status. Although jittery about the pending punishment, she was also stimulated by her own submissiveness.

He prowled closely behind. She could sense his excitement. "Because of your misbehavior, I get the pleasure of finishing what we started three weeks ago."

Lyndsey shuddered, her pelvis clenching impossibly tighter.

"How does that make you feel?" He twirled a lock of her hair around his finger.

*Don't ask me that*, she cried silently. Embarrassment came next, adding a new flavor to her arousal.

Before she could answer, Damien twisted her hair tighter and tugged. "You must always tell me the truth. Honesty is another important part of a D/s relationship. You may not fully understand it yet, but, as I've said, you have all the power. Your submission is a gift to me but can be revoked at any time. I get to play with your body and take pleasure in controlling you, and believe me I'll enjoy every minute of it, but only so long as that's what you desire. In this way, you are really the one in control. And none of that works without absolute honesty between us."

He released her hair and turned her to face him.

"I understand, I think."

He raised an eyebrow and waited. When she didn't grasp the issue, Damien added, "We're in a training phase of our relationship, so I'll help train you to remember to use Sir by administering the crop every time you forget."

Lyndsey yelped and jumped back.

He laughed. "I haven't even touched you yet."

"I'm sorry, Sir. I'll try to remember...Sir." She threw in the second for good measure.

Lyndsey watched as he selected a crop from the many hanging on the wall. He forcefully slashed it through the air, making it whistle. Next, he selected a leather paddle, and smacked it hard against his hand. Lyndsey jumped at the harsh sound.

"The first ten will be your punishment. The rest will be for my pleasure."

"What?" Lyndsey tensed, barely stopping herself from bolting.

He strode back to her, shaking his head as if disappointed in her.

She shouted too-late. "Sir!"

Damien whispered directly into her ear, the sound washing over her like a soothing caress. "Now I'm going to strap your beautiful naked body down to the bench and spank your bare ass with the sting of the paddle and the kiss of the crop. When you melt for me, and I think you will, I'm going to play with your body. I'll fondle and caress and tease until you're pleading for me to take you. Turn you into an incoherent, mindless fuck toy, begging to be allowed to come. I won't stop until you're offering to do any naughty, depraved act I want, just to get off."

A tremulous gasp slipped from her lips at his obscene teasing. Electricity quivered out from her pelvis to the ends of every limb. Swaying toward him, so close Lyndsey could feel his heat, she shuddered violently, overwhelming lust beyond anything she'd ever before experienced slammed into her. But it made her feel wonderful, a fully-alive, sexual being for the first time in her life.

"Now," his voice strong and stern. "Tell me how you feel?"

He really was going to make her admit that the thought of him spanking her was arousing. That his debasing words excited strange parts of her. Again, mortification surged, and Lyndsey took in a deep fortifying breath. Several. Stalling.

It was clear that he understood her, knew what would make her feel feminine and needy, and she found that reassuring. At last, she would find that elusive nirvana, would not have to fake it. It was Damien who had brought her to this Land of Oz, and, while it was a strange and fantastical place, full of odd equipment and strange customs, she was sure of one thing. With him, she had found a wizard who would master her and take her places she could never go on her own.

He'd waited quietly and she knew it was time. Time to submit, completely and with her whole heart. Time to lay herself bare before him. And she wanted to bare herself to him more than she would have thought possible.

"Sir, when you talk like that I get aroused," her timbre a barely-there breathy whisper. She'd managed to say it, but a fresh flush of mortification made her face hot.

"You're delightful when you blush." He sounded pleased, even though she couldn't bring herself to look at him. Standing so close but not touching her, he urged "Tell me more. Describe it. Describe where on your body you feel horny."

She gasped. "I can't. Sir."

"You can. And will." He slammed his hand down on the leather bench, the smack reverberating loudly through the room.

Lyndsey jumped but it was nothing compared to how tightly her pussy clenched, hungrily.

"Um…I feel dizzy, and hot, and like I can't get enough air." It wasn't what he wanted to hear, or at least not enough, she guessed.

Lyndsey breathed in deeply, trying to calm herself, and tried again. "My palms feel moist, and my knees feel weak, and my breasts feel heavy, tingly."

"Good. More."

It was so hard to tell him all her wicked secret desires, but Damien wanted her complete submission, not just her body but her mind too.

Lyndsey shut her eyes for a second so she could concentrate on the myriad sensations. "My lips want to kiss you and…and…" In a rush, she got it all out before humiliation could shut her down. "And my tits ache and my pussy keeps clenching, almost pulsing, but in a good way, and I'm wet and dizzy with lust and…please, Sir!" she wailed.

"Beautiful," he murmured. "Now tell me what you want me to do about it."

Lyndsey whimpered. It was debasing and arousing at the same time. Her pulse raced and she panted, and he hadn't even touched her.

Yet.

*Slam.* His hand hit the bench again.

Lyndsey lurched, fight or flight reactions zinging around her body, making her crazy, hyperaware. The air in the room felt tangible, like the brush of soft velvet upon her bare skin. The cold slate floor under her bare feet enhanced the ancient feel of the dungeon and her lowly position. She could even feel his body heat, so close, but she didn't dare reach out. She could smell him too—a spicy, manly musk that she was beginning to recognize as distinctly Damien.

However, she desperately wanted to understand his dominance, try to catch a glimmer of what made him her kryptonite. And he was that for her—her body so weak for his touch, her lust his to mold, and deep within her, a blossoming itch to serve him in any way he desired.

*Was this what it was to be a submissive?*

"Tell me specifically, in detail, what you hope I'll do to you this pleasant afternoon." Somehow her arousal spiked even higher. It made no sense, but there was no denying it.

But how could she possibly put her kinky thoughts into words? Tell him her secret fantasies. The ones that had been building exponentially since she'd met him. It was too much.

It was also clear that nothing was going to happen until she revealed her dark cravings. And she wanted things to happen. She wanted all of it to happen. To her. On her. It all hinged on her ability to be brave enough to say what she needed.

With effort, Lyndsey forced the words out, as if talking through a thick, choking fog. "Sir, I want everything you said. *Everything.* Even the stuff I don't know about yet. I want…" She sucked in a harsh breath and tried again. "I want to be tied down, unable to resist you, unable to stop you from doing whatever you want. I want to be spanked. By that paddle or even the crop and, especially, I want to feel your hand on my ass. Like the bench felt your hand. Hard. Loud."

There was a moment of silence.

"Fuck me," he swore under his breath.

Lyndsey couldn't look at him, her eyes locked on the floor, ashamed about admitting that she wanted these things done to her. At the same time, his reaction gratified her.

"Describe what else you want?" His commanding tone was back.

She started to sweat, her palms moist. Her chest tightened, and she couldn't breathe. Above all, a bitch-in-heat hunger choked her. So fucking aroused, Lyndsey thought she might faint. Through the shimmering lust, she began to understand that even this crazy talk was foreplay, Master Edge style.

She had to see his face, had to know what he was thinking. Slowly, Lyndsey raised her eyes to meet his and saw hunger, caring, reassurance, and, above all, strength. The eyes of a dominant, they urged her forward. "Sir, I liked the idea of you playing with my body, teasing me. Even making me beg. I'm already so turned on, I think I'll explode. I can't wait to feel you inside me."

"Pretty woman, you're going to get everything you want, but first you earned the coming punishment when you trespassed, and when you failed to read the posted warning, and when you nearly ran from me, and when you didn't trust me. I am thrilled that you're here with me, that you want me as much as I want you, but with me there are rules and submission and everything that goes with a D/s relationship. What do you say?"

There it was again. The line that must be crossed, as bright and rosy-red as her spanked ass would soon be. She'd been edging toward it for three weeks, ever since she'd stumbled upon this place. To be with him meant crossing the line into his kinky world.

After taking a deep breath, she whispered the difficult words, "Please punish me, Sir."

She tilted her head down, deferentially lowering her gaze, and waited for instructions.

He replied in a voice hoarse with lust, ordering her to climb onto the equipment. Within minutes, she found her upper body and arms secured to the bench and a blindfold shuttering her vision. Fresh embarrassment barreled through her when he placed his hands on the backs of her thighs and pushed them wide apart, cool air rushing across her moist hot flesh. He secured them to the kneelers, and no matter how she tried, she couldn't close her legs. She remained vulnerable and open to him.

From behind, his hand slipped between her legs and he drew his fingers along her pussy. "So delightfully wet." She moaned, the feel of his hand more enticing than the mortification was humiliating.

"Punishment first," he decreed. It sounded so matter of fact, this medieval justice he was about to administer.

His bare hand landed on her buttocks in swift forceful succession. Over and over, he rained down reprimands, while counting, "One, two, three, four."

"Ouch," she cried out, involuntarily. "That hurts." She'd expected that, but…

Chuckling quietly, he continued. "Five, six, seven, eight."

"Shit! It hurts," she squealed again.

"Language," he warned, continuing to rain down urgent correction on her ass.

Lyndsey twisted and turned, thrashing about to escape the barrage, but it was useless. She was trussed like a pig to slaughter. And he was slaughtering her.

"Eighteen, nineteen, twenty," he counted. "There. That's the worst of it."

Over her panting, Lyndsey could hear him strip off his shirt. No longer fighting the restraints, she collapsed onto the bench. Lightheaded, she tried to catch her breath while also trying to calm her thoughts about what had just happened.

She remembered then what he'd said. "The worst of it? Sir."

"I'm not done with you. Just the punishment phase. Now comes pleasurable pain."

"But, Sir," she wailed, turning her face toward him even though still blindfolded. "You can't believe that more spankings will feel good."

"Ah. A challenge," his voice by far too lighthearted. "I can never back down from a challenge."

"That's not what I meant," Lyndsey snapped.

Swifter than she could have imagined, a crop landed on her ass, leaving a stinging slice of fire.

"Always address me as Sir. You mustn't forget the niceties."

Lyndsey growled. Loudly. Feeling rather more like an angry bull than a meek hog.

Then she felt it. Damien's hand, trailing up her inner thigh and heading toward the goods.

*No!* she yelled silently. He'd discover the truth. Uselessly, she tried to close her thighs.

"Mm-hm." The sound was supreme male satisfaction as his seeking hand found soaking wet her. His fingers slipped easily inside. "I think the melting has commenced," he teased. Damien fondled her, spreading the moisture all over her private places, while she panted and tried to find her equilibrium.

"Oh," she exclaimed. His fingers had found her clit and were alternately caressing and flicking it. Lyndsey transformed into a squirming, moaning, primitive creature, but now for pleasure instead of pain.

"I paid a lot of attention, last night," he told her quietly as his exploring fingers unerringly did amazing things to her. "I'm a very good student, you'll find out. I'll soon know every secret your body holds." She heard him kick off his shoes and wondered if he was undressing even as his magical hands continued to play across her body.

Lyndsey agreed, as at that moment she was edging toward a climax. Never had she gotten so far so quickly, as the delicious sensations built and built. She no longer cared that she was strapped down. That he'd spanked her. That she was in sex slave training. All the mattered was the magic he was creating in her body.

And then it stopped.

"No. Please, Sir."

Damien laughed. "Don't worry, I'm not through with you."

She listened, trying to hear what he was about.

"Remember your safe word, if you need it."

A band of brilliant fire sliced across her ass.

Lyndsey screamed. It stung a blue streak, but her arousal spiked higher too.

Two more times fiery lashes seared her, and two more times Lyndsey shrieked. She thrashed about, trying ineffectively to avoid the pain.

*It's too much!* Damien was pushing her too hard, pushing past boundaries she didn't know she had. The safe word he'd given her rose to her lips, but she hesitated. It would disappoint Master. Without conscious choice, she'd put him there in that place of ultimate power. Using her safe word to control him would lessen his supremacy, and she didn't want that, didn't want anything that would make him anything less than her absolute Master.

Another white-hot slice landed across her backside and Lyndsey shrieked. Then cried out.

*"Master!"* Her wail echoed in the dungeon.

It was a plea and an endearment and tears started to form in her eyes. Not from the sting, but from the rightness of calling him Master. Damien had been correct all along. Here, alone with him, playing and fucking, she was indeed a sexual submissive. She knew it now down to her bones. And to her burning ass.

And that was okay. Her right, as an adult, to explore whatever part of herself she wished.

She was utterly, gloriously, wholeheartedly horny. Her body was on fire…for his touch alone.

Tense and alert, Lyndsey panted, but no more agony fell. She heard the subtle sound of the crop hitting the floor.

Then Master was there, she could feel his presence next to her, if not his body. He trailed a tingling line of soft kisses down her back, and his hand gently traced a line up her leg from ankle to thigh and finally to her buttocks. She tightened, waiting for another stroke, but instead he massaged her heated flesh.

Lyndsey moaned, her entire body on overdrive. His every touch or lick or even the caress of his breath on her electrified skin, built the fire within her.

He put his lips at her ear. "You honor me," his voice thick with lust. "I've long been called Master Edge, but I never wanted to be anyone's master."

Lyndsey's heart dropped. She opened her mouth to take it back. Apologize.

"Until now," he whispered.

Master whipped off her blindfold and caught her gaze with his where her head lay on the bench. She could see the sincerity in his eyes. "From you, it fills a place inside me that makes me complete."

Lyndsey's heart was so full she almost couldn't breathe.

His arrogant masculinity was back in the slight quirk of his sexy grin and the sinful gleam of his regard. He grasped her hair, wrapping it around his hand, and forcefully lifted her face just enough to claim her mouth with his. He demanded her full surrender, and she gave it to him, opening her mouth to his invading tongue. He sought hers out, played with her, and seemed to silently declare, "Mine, all mine."

"Yes," she breathed into his mouth, even though he hadn't spoken. "Please, Master."

He pulled away and rose. She watched him rapidly don a condom like a man possessed and within seconds was standing behind the bench, moving into the space between her spread legs. And, finally, Master was inside her. Fully insider her, tip to balls.

He groaned with deep satisfaction, thrilling Lyndsey that she could bring him such bliss.

"Yes," she sang joyfully.

"Yes," he grunted, pulling almost all the way out and pushing home again.

Master began to thrust forcefully, really pound into her, as if he were lost in the sensations and unable to control himself. Lyndsey loved seeing him like this and loved the feel of him taking his pleasure in her. Driving into her over and over, each time going deeper, filling her fuller.

She tried to raise her hips to meet him, but the strap across her back held her prisoner. Master saw what she attempted and stopped moving altogether, his chuckle in the air.

"They don't call me Master Edge for nothing."

He began to move again, but now he was toying with her. Master seemed to have complete control of his hunger, repeatedly building them both up to a point just shy of ecstasy and then slowing them down. Captive to his game, writhing but unable to find release, her body silently screamed in protest. Again and again, Master took them to the brink.

Built them up.

Faster, stronger, deeper.

Relentless. Pushing until Lyndsey was mindlessly riding the crest, the climax tantalizingly imminent, just beyond her reach.

Then...

Slowing them down.

Barely moving.

Pausing altogether.

The raw itch, pure torture. The need to explode, brutal.

Lyndsey squirmed and moaned and begged incoherently. "Please, Master. Please!"

"You're amazing and so beautiful, my sub," he murmured, and her pussy contracted around his cock. *"My* sub," he repeated, warmly.

Lyndsey almost missed the inflection, so lost was she in a sea of blind, unending desire as he ramped up the mind-blowing friction again, but somehow his claiming of her vaguely registered. She was his and he was hers, in ways she couldn't have imagined just a month ago. It electrified her. Her entire body flamed hotter.

Faster and faster, he fucked her. Finally, Master seemed to lose control too, so wild and abandoned his thrusting became.

He shouted, "Now come for me."

His dominance set her off like a rocket. Lyndsey exploded, shuddering in a frenzy of pleasure. Delicious electricity shot through her in wave after wave of ecstasy. Master pushed her farther, forcing more pleasure as he continued to love her with his body until she was utterly spent, floating on a delirious river of bliss.

Master joined her there, thrusting his pelvis into her one last time. "Yes," he grunted, before juddering to a stop deep inside her, their bodies locked together, two lovers made one. Locked together in sweet euphoria.

Master collapsed down onto her, his sweat-slicked chest on her damp back. For a few minutes, they rested, until their panting subsided.

Damien rose and removed her restraints. He helped her off the spanking bench and swept her into his arms, carrying her to the luxurious bed that awaited them, the covers already pulled back. The careful way he placed her on the bed showed her that she was precious to him. After joining her and pulling up the blanket, he drew her close, into the crook of his arm.

"Thank you," he murmured into her ear. "You honor me with your presence and your giving nature."

Lyndsey giggled. "But you love it too when I call you Master, don't you?"

In the dim afternoon light filtering in through the curtains, she could see the broad grin spread across his face.

"Of course, I do. And you like it when I call you my sub." It wasn't a question.

"How do you know that?" Curiosity winning over any face-saving denial.

"Your pussy clenched down on my dick every time I said it." He smirked at her.

Lyndsey wanted to smack that look of arrogance right off his face, but instead she leaned closer and kissed him on the lips. "You're so full of it."

"Have you learned nothing?" he asked in mock severity. "You must always say, Sir, when you denigrate me. Now where did I leave that crop?"

"Okay. Okay. I'll be good…Sir."

"Seriously, I wouldn't be a good Dom if I wasn't paying close attention to your every reaction. Learning about you, from the punishment and the pleasure. What works and doesn't. And,"—he leaned in and nuzzled her nose playfully with his— "I just learned a whole lot about you, sweet Lyndsey."

She nuzzled him back. Her hands finally free to explore, she trailed her fingers across his chest and lower.

And lower.

He stopped her before she reached the goods.

"Want more, do you?" he laughed. "But first, as your new Master, I need to ask you what you'll do next time you're upset and unsure. About us. About BDSM. About anything." It was clear from his quiet demeanor, that he was serious, although the mischief in his eyes returned when he added, "Of course, I don't mind *teaching* you as many times as it takes until you've learned my rules."

Lyndsey's ass still smarted from his "teaching," her hand reflexively moving back to protect it. "No, Sir. I learned that one already. I promise to always come to you, if I have a problem. Or at least let you know if I need time to think." It was a slim boundary to her independence, but she drew it nonetheless. "And I won't do anything to make you worry about my welfare."

"That's all I ask." He nuzzled her again.

Lyndsey resumed exploring him with her hands, loving the contours of his built chest, his chiseled abs, the hair just above his...

This time, it didn't seem he would stop her from finding the goods. Lyndsey played in the tight curls there, shy of going farther, but she could tell from his harsh breath and tightening abdomen he was affected by her touch.

She leaned up to kiss his chest, finding his nipple and licking.

"Mm." She smiled, her mouth still on him, happy he was letting her play.

A thought occurred to her. Was this all there was to it? She just needed follow his rules and that was that. Something akin to a letdown settled in her stomach, rather than pride of accomplishment and relief at no more punishment. *Is this all there is?*

"Does this mean, I'm all trained?" She had to know.

He laughed, a big deep belly one. "No, my sweet novice, this is just the beginning."

"Oh. What else?" she asked quickly.

He laughed again. "You're an eager little thing, aren't you? I'm not going to share all my secret plans for you, but know this, when I'm done you'll know as much about pleasing me sexually as I'm learning about you. Some of it you might find difficult, you might have to learn to like." His hand slid behind between her buttocks to touch her anus, hinting at one item that might be on the difficult list. "But I'll always put your care and needs first."

The thought of Master training her to serve him sexually set her body on fire yet again, but for once Lyndsey didn't fight it, having finally accepted her submissive yearnings. Would he teach her those obscene sub postures she'd read about online? Would he tie her up in intricate knots designed to tease or torture all her erogenous zones? Would she learn how to deep throat or take him in the ass or any of those other erotic practices she once thought debasing? And, would she disobey his rules just so he'd have to punish her? Lastly, would Master want to…

Lyndsey's contemplations slammed to a halt. Remembering the slaves she'd seen here and what she'd read online conjured a new image. The ultimate sign of ownership loomed over her.

"Will you, when I'm all trained—" She shut her mouth, afraid she wouldn't like the answer. Afraid he wouldn't want such a big commitment. Wouldn't want her that much.

Master made a tsking sound, shaking his head slightly, but she could see that he was amused. "Novice, you aren't breaking your promise already?"

Lyndsey swallowed. She wasn't entirely sure what she wanted from him. Did she really want that?

"I'm getting the crop." Although, he smiled at her too.

Damien pushed back the covers, and Lyndsey grabbed his arm and blurted, "Will you collar me? Make me your true sex slave?"

She held her breath.

"Once your training is complete and if that is what you want, I would love to put a collar around your neck. Within our dungeon, wherever that is or whatever form that takes, I would love nothing better than to become your Master in every kinky sense."

"But only in the dungeon, right?"

"Right."

The air rushed out of her chest in a whoosh, relief telling her that no matter how strange or new or depraved it seemed— at least in the eyes of some people—her Master had said what she most wanted to hear. He wished to claim her in that monumental and meaningful way.

Damien turned to face her and took both her hands in his, squeezing them reassuringly. "Lyndsey, I really like you. Everything about you. In and out of the dungeon. And, when we're ready, we'll take that step in a private ceremony among kinksters or just us if you prefer. And after that, we'll take the next step. And the next, because even though we're a brand new couple, I already can't imagine you not being in my life. I hope…"

A look of uncertainty filled his expression.

Lyndsey launched herself at him, throwing her arms around his neck. "Yes, Damien, Yes! I like you too, and also Master Edge. So very much! *My* very own Master."

Lyndsey kissed him full on with everything she had, and Damien pulled her to him tightly. Tenderly.

And they kissed and kissed, until they weren't just kissing anymore.

Until they were intertwined and pulsing and making love. Locked together.

Two lovers made one.

Dear Reader,

Thank you for reading my story. I hope you enjoyed it and if you did, could you please take a moment to leave me a review on Amazon, Goodreads, or your favorite retailer? I hope to meet you at a book signing sometime soon!

With my thanks,

Kate

KEEP READING FOR A SAMPLE OF KATE'S LATEST RELEASE FROM ENTANGLED PUBLISHING...

# Her Gentleman Dom

## *Chapter 1: Drafting*

---

*"...firmness, commodity, and delight."*
*—Essential architectural qualities as defined by Vitruvius,*
*circa 27 B.C.*

*God, he's hot.*

Her hands stilled, her breath caught, and she stopped listening.

Lillian Victoria West had watched the newcomer walk to the podium to shake the hand of Drake Design Group's senior partner. Introduced as their newest star architect, Finlay Hyde came from London, with an outstanding pedigree.

*Come on already!* Lilli wanted them to get on with announcing the contest winner, but she applauded politely along with everyone else in the large conference room, while Hyde shook the other partners' hands, his back to her.

But then he'd turned and smiled.

And her world had tilted.

Lilli's pulse raced and her chest tightened, like she couldn't breathe.

He definitely looked British in his tweed jacket and slightly disheveled baggy chinos, but it was his quirky, Jude Law-esque grin that threw her into chaos. His tousled light, brown hair that made her want to do something crazy, like go up to him and run her hands through his tawny curls.

Lilli wasn't looking for a guy, didn't even have a Tinder account, but her attraction to him blasted her like wind off the San Francisco bay.

She quietly hugged herself, applying pressure to her shoulders, needing the grounding such contact gave her. She tried not to squirm, but the chair was uncomfortable for the high-rent, high-rise offices. Or maybe it was him that made her so antsy.

Hyde stepped up to the podium and, in cultured tones that spoke of wealth and status, thanked Drake for the opportunity. "I'm chuffed to be here, and I must say I feel right at home with all this beastly weather." Chuckles echoed around the room, given that it was a typical Fog City day.

Arms still wrapped around herself, she leaned forward, trying to see what color his eyes were behind his expensive horn-rimmed glasses. He was the quintessential representation of a nerdy but handsome Englishman. He looked older, maybe forty, but that didn't lessen his appeal. A small grin played across her face as she enjoyed a moment of anonymous admiration from her spot in the third row. Although she didn't date much, too busy with her career, Lilli had "a type," and that type was standing before her.

While Hyde spoke about his goals at the firm, his words held her spellbound. Not their meaning, but his British accent that sounded at once foreign, formal, and flirty. It washed over her with the tangy sensuality of an English ale drunk on a hot summer day. Her eyes drifted shut, and an image of a large plush bed sprang to her mind, Finlay whispering sexy things into her ear as they lay naked and tangled upon it.

Lilli's eyes popped open. *Where did that come from?*

"It is my privilege to announce…"

She tried to focus, but heat flushed her skin. Her thighs closed, clenched, and she sucked in several breaths of cooling air. Applause sounded around her. Without thought she joined in, her hands patting slowly together like a winding-down automaton. His mouth moved, but she didn't hear the words, his lips—their dusky rose color and enticing contours—seizing her attention.

"As we say across the pond, I am absolutely chuffed about this deserving project. So, I hope the winner is here today. Again, would Miss Lillian West please come forward?"

Louder applause startled her back into the moment. It felt like she was waking from an erotic dream. Everyone was glancing around until the general milieu settled on her, the senior partner pointing her way. Lilli rose and looked about in confusion.

*Oh, shoot. What did I miss?*

"Come on up, Ms. West," Hyde said, encouraging her forward with his hand.

*Did I win?*

Giving her head a little shake, she sidled out of her row and moved forward, focusing on the senior partner to avoid ogling Mr. Sex-on-a-Stick.

Her eyes darted over anyway. Hyde smiled at her, but the twinkle in his eyes suggested he was amused by her curious conduct.

"Congratulations, Ms. West," said Mr. Drake, shaking her hand. Lilli gave him what she hoped was a grateful smile, distracted as she was.

Hyde came next, but when her fingers touched his, electricity, hot and energetic, shot up her arm, spreading fire through her body. Her eyes rose to his, and he quirked a naughty grin, an eyebrow raised, as if he knew exactly what she was feeling. She pulled her hand back too abruptly and forced her gaze to Mr. Drake, who started speaking to the audience.

"We're pleased we can assist the Fresh Start Training Center, a neighborhood-based program that provides free job training assistance for the unemployed, something much needed in the Hunter's Point area."

More applause followed.

Mr. Drake led her to the microphone. She looked out at everyone, a dazed smile on her face. She hoped that any remaining Fresh Start board members who still harbored doubts about hiring a such young woman to helm an important organization would at last be satisfied. Lilli's tentative smile surged into a beaming, ecstatic grin as her full triumph hit her.

"Thank you so much to all the partners at DDG. Winning this prestigious competition will make raising the remaining building funds much easier. Thank you."

After the press conference concluded, Lilli was invited to stand with the firm's top staff for a photo op. She was ever aware of Hyde's presence next to her.

As people filed out of the room, Mr. Drake turned to her and Hyde. "What do you say, Finn? Think you can do this little lady a good turn? Transform a derelict building into a useful space. On budget and on time."

*What? Wait.*

Lilli's gaze swung from the elderly man to the gorgeous Brit. He seemed friendly, if somewhat overly polite in that English way, but her anxiety shot up at the realization she'd have to maintain a professional demeanor with Mr. Sex-on-a-Stick. Her feeling of triumph wobbled, like one of the stairs in the run-down building that had been donated to her nonprofit.

"I'm looking forward to the challenge," Hyde answered.

His gaze caught hers and locked her to him, his wide grin exuding confidence and authority. Meeting his smile with her own, Lilli's chin notched up a little higher.

"I can't thank you all enough." She spoke a little too loudly, attempting to cover a strange, skittish energy that made her want to squirm. *What the heck is wrong with me?* Even her palm still felt hot from their brief handshake.

"Congratulations again, Ms. West," Drake said, starting to turn away. "I'll leave you both to it, then."

Hyde stepped near, obliging her to tilt her head back to look up at him. "We're going to work well together. I'm sure of it." The low dulcet timbre of his voice sparked yet another warm tingle that traveled down her spine all the way to her toes.

Standing this close, Lilli could see that his eyes were green, an amazing shade of hazel with flecks of burnt auburn on the edges, fringed with dark, thick lashes. Again, she longed to reach up and remove his expensive glasses for a better look.

*Get ahold of yourself,* Lilli thought.

"Why don't we go to my office and get started talking over some preliminaries?"

Lilli nodded, mouth closed, not trusting her voice to sound strong and professional. Every time he smiled down at her, she grew warmer, knees weaker. This was the first time she'd had an immediate and overwhelming reaction to a man, and she didn't know how to handle the feelings coursing through her.

*Don't blow it,* she repeated over and over while Hyde escorted her down the long hallway to his corner office. Her entire career hinged on this. She surreptitiously pressed a hand to her thigh, needing the grounding sensation.

# *Chapter 2: Functional Specifications*

---

Finn watched the nervous young woman while she talked about her project goals. She sat, pert and upright, opposite him, across his elegant glass desk, while he relaxed back. The delectable Miss West had dressed for success—boxy suit, simple makeup, businesslike hairstyle—but underneath her professional facade she was exquisite. Stunning even.

"Thank you for this opportunity," she repeated for the third time. She fluttered her hands about as she gushed, before clasping them together and forcing them onto her lap, as if realizing how she was behaving. Her jittery aura, shy but energetic, stirred something in him and generated an immediate, almost primal, reaction.

Lust. Excitement. The hunger to hunt.

The feelings were not wanted. Beginning an affair with his pro bono client on his first assignment was a nonstarter. Finn dragged his gaze away to the floor-to-ceiling windows. *Dog's bollocks!* He had finally made it. Finally achieved the success he'd been working so hard for. The right to choose his projects. Huge salary. Fancy office with a view. Swiveling back toward her, Finn leaned forward on his Herman Miller Aeron and tried to focus *only* on what Miss West was saying and not on her other delicious attributes.

"It will mean a great deal to the unemployed in the neighborhood." Her voice had a lush, sweet quality, reminding him of a ripe berry, ready to be savored.

Earnest and eager, she leaned toward Finn. "I am really so *very* grateful."

"Just how grateful are you willing to be?" He hadn't meant to say it aloud, but amusement made his mouth curl up at the corners.

"I'll do absolutely any— Wait. Excuse me?"

Miss West's chocolate brown eyes widened. Framed by sooty lashes, they blinked as she seemed to process his words. "I'm sorry, what did you say?"

He should let her off the hook, as Americans would say, but he was having too much fun. "I think you heard me."

Lilli's mouth parted into a little "o," and his gaze settled on her rosy lips. Lush, utterly kissable lips that made him hungry for a taste. Again, ripe berries came to mind.

"I…ah, um."

"Yes, Miss West?" Finn nodded, adopting a mask of serious interest.

"It must be that you're foreign. I mean, it's just that here, in this country, what you said might sound like…"

"Like?" Finn lured her, loving the game because playing cat and mouse was his specialty. Because the pets he usually played with always loved it when he caught them.

"Um." She looked adorable. Cornered. "Like you expected…wanted…" A blush spread across her face and her chest rose and fell.

His body tensed, desire jolting him in the gut. He jerked back from the hot pull of her gaze. *Bloody fuck!* His secret game had backfired, and he was caught in a snare of his own making.

Finn sighed. He loved games, but not with naive, unsuspecting young women. He'd forfeit rather than make her any more uncomfortable.

"Miss West, let me clarify. I meant only that I'll need you to put your full effort into making this project a success. Quick turnaround on approvals. Meeting deadlines. That sort of thing."

"Oh." She breathed it out like the low note in a love song. Then her eyes grew huge. "How stupid of me. Of course, that's all you meant."

Her gaze, that moments ago had smoldered, now darted away toward the window. She rose and hurried to the thick glass, the dissipated fog revealing the sparkling blue waters far below.

"What an amazing view of the Golden Gate Bridge."

He joined her there, looking outward. It gave Finn some time to talk himself down. She was a client. She was too young, barely mid-twenties, he guessed. Most of all, her reticence marked her as too innocent to ever meet his needs.

*She is not for you.*

A movement caught his eye. She was taking deep, slow breaths, almost as if she were counting them. But it was her hands pressing against her thighs, molding the fabric of her skirt to her legs, that made his body stir again. Interesting. He doubted Miss Lilli West realized how much she looked like a sex slave standing at attention, the first pose he taught any trainee.

*She is not for you.*

Needing to get back on track, he asked her about the history of the old building that was the foundation of the project.

With apparent effort, Lilli dragged her gaze from the view to look at Finn. Her luminous eyes blinked and stared at him, seeming confused. "It's…um…a unique structure with period features that…um…" Her voice trailed off, and they stared at each other, instinctively leaning closer.

He could smell her now, a light, floral perfume. Underneath, notes of something musky that he guessed was her unique scent. He took a deep breath while he studied her face, and she watched him, alert but not wary. That was good.

The silence between them stretched on until Finn broke it with a slight cough. "Miss West, at this point, I would like to schedule a walk-through to see the site myself."

"Of course. Whatever you need." Bubbling over with yet more thanks to him and DDG, her hand landing on his shoulder for emphasis. "I can't wait to serve you in *any* way I can."

Her subservience, however innocent, was manna to his inner Dom. Surging adrenaline made him stand taller, made his blood come alive. He felt her hand like a hot brand. His subs knew better than to touch him without permission, would do so only if they wanted to be taken over his knee. She didn't, but instinct made his hands prickle for a chance at her bare ass.

Finn reached for her hand still on his arm—unsure whether he would hold it, remove it, or use it to pull her over his knee…

# Her Gentleman Dom

## PUBLICATION DATE - 10/15/18

### AVAILABLE IN PRINT & EBOOK FROM AMAZON

## Other books by Kate Allure

*Bed & Breakfast & Bondage*

*Her Gentleman Dom*

*Lawyer Up*

*Laying Pipe*

*Playing Doctor*

## Subscribe to Kate's Newsletter at:

**www.kateallure.com**

Twitter: @KateAllure

Facebook.com/KateAllure.Sizzling.Romance

Pinterest.com/KateAllure

https://www.instagram.com/kate.allure

## Acknowledgements

Thank you to all who helped with this novel. First, I must thank my sweet, sexy, and supportive graphic designer (who also happens to be my husband) as well as my close friend, critique partner Anna. As always, I'm grateful for the encouragement of my agent Louise Fury of The Bent Agency. I also offer a shout out to family and friends for their support and, most importantly, to all of you who took the time to read this novel. I'm thankful and hope that you enjoyed it!

## About the Author

Kate Allure writes erotic romances that celebrate sensuality, sexual exploration and, of course, true love. Writing for Entangled Publishing and Sourcebooks, her books feature real women meeting handsome professional, working men as they go about their everyday lives—and the fun they have behind closed doors! Her work is "Escapism of the richest, most decadent variety," 4 Stars (*RT Book Reviews*), and "sizzling and sensual. Intense chemistry, great characterization, and a kinky page-singeing ending will have readers clamoring for more," (*Publishers Weekly*). Kate's non-fiction writing included working for American Ballet Theatre and New York City Ballet, and recently creating the *Romance Readers Guide to Historic London* under the name Sonja Rouillard. Beyond writing, Kate's passions include traveling and exploring all things sensual with her loving husband.

### BDSM disclaimer for my readers ~

You've all seen the silly TV ads where a racecar driver performs some stunt and at the bottom it reads, "Professional driver, closed course—Do Not Attempt." This is that…do not try this stuff at home. Do not try the BDSM acts in my stories unless you know what you're doing, have a safe partner, and take responsibility for your actions. Specifically, B&B&B2 is a fictional story that explores BDSM and the practices inherent in the lifestyle. It is not intended to be a how-to manual or advocate that anyone try anything described here. This author and publisher take no legal responsibility for any results of anyone attempting to copy the sexual acts depicted in the story. Lastly, I believe wholeheartedly that everyone should follow the SSC code—Safe, Sane, and Consensual.